Rude Tales and Glorious

"IN ALL THAT SWIRLING SEA OF CHAOS THERE WAS BUT ONE ISLAND OF COMFORT, THE STURDY CASTLE OF DOLBADARN."

RUDE TALES AND GLORIOUS

BEING: THE ONLY TRUE ACCOUNT
OF DIVERSE FEATS OF BRAWN
AND BAWD PERFORMED BY
KING ARTHUR AND HIS
KNIGHTS OF THE
TABLE ROUND

DAVYDD AP SEARE
VIA
NICHOLAS SEARE

ILLUSTRATED BY
WILLIAM BRAMHALL

CLARKSON N. POTTER, INC./ PUBLISHERS, NEW YORK
DISTRIBUTED BY CROWN PUBLISHERS, INC.
1 9 8 3

PUBLISHED BY CLARKSON N. POTTER, INC.,
ONE PARK AVENUE, NEW YORK, NEW YORK 10016
AND SIMULTANEOUSLY IN CANADA BY
GENERAL PUBLISHING COMPANY LIMITED

MANUFACTURED IN THE UNITED STATES OF AMERICA

LIBRARY OF CONGRESS CATALOGING IN PUBLICATION DATA
SEARE, NICHOLAS.
RUDE TALES AND GLORIOUS.
1. ARTHURIAN ROMANCES. I. TITLE.
PS3569.E1763R8   1983   813'.54   82-24019
ISBN 0-517-54986-7

DESIGN BY GAEL TOWEY DILLON
ILLUSTRATIONS BY WILLIAM BRAMHALL
10 9 8 7 6 5 4 3 2 1
FIRST EDITION

*THIS TRANSLATION IS DEDICATED
TO THE GUIDING SHADES OF:*

GEOFFREY, MIGUEL, GIOVANNI, AND FRANÇOIS.

INTRODUCTION

In ages when there were no books, when noblemen and princes themselves could not read, history or tradition was monopolized by the story-tellers. They inherited, generation after generation, the wonderous tales of their predecessors, which they retailed to the public with such additions of their own as their acquired information supplied them with. Anachronisms became of course very common, and errors of geography, of locality, of manners, equally so. Spurious genealogies were invented, in which Arthur and his knights were made to derive their descent from Aeneas, Hector, or some other of the Trojan heroes.

At a time when chivalry excited universal admiration, it was natural that literature should receive the same impulse, and that history and fable should be ransacked to furnish examples of courage and piety that might excite increased emulation. Arthur and Charlemagne were the two heroes selected for this purpose. Arthur's pretensions were that he was a brave, though not always a successful warrior, and the Britons carried with them into Wales the memory of his exploits, which their national vanity insensibly exaggerated, until the little prince of the Silures (South

Wales) was magnified into the conqueror of England, of Gaul, and of the greater part of Europe. His gene-alogy was gradually carried up to an imaginary Brutus, and to the period of the Trojan war, and a sort of chronicle was composed in the Welsh, or Armorican language, which, under the pompous title of the *History of the Kings of Britain,* was translated into Latin by Geoffrey of Monmouth, about the year 1150. The Welsh critics consider the material of the work to have been an older history, written by St. Talian, Bishop of St. Asaph, in the seventh century.

These fabulous chronicles were for a while im-prisoned in languages of local only or of professional access. They might be read by ecclesiastics, the sole Latin scholars of those times, and Geoffrey's British original would contribute to the gratification of Welshmen; but neither could become extensively popular till translated into some language of general and familiar use.

The earliest form in which the romances appear is that of a rude kind of verse. In this form, it is sup-posed they were sung or recited at the feasts of princes and knights in their baronial halls.

It was not till towards the end of the thirteenth century that the prose romances began to appear. These works generally began with disowning and dis-crediting the sources from which in reality they drew their sole information. As every romance was sup-posed to be a real history, compilers of those in prose would have forfeited all credit if they had announced themselves as mere copyists of the minstrels. On the contrary, they usually state that, as the popular poems upon the matter in question contain many "lesings," they had been induced to translate the real and true history of such or such a knight from the original Latin or Greek, or from the ancient British or Armorican authorities, which authorities existed only in their own assertion.

> From *Mythology: The Age of Chivalry*
> by Thomas Bulfinch (1796–1867)

P R E F A C E

Through all the generations of the Seares, an impulse towards scholarship has been a kind of inherited genetic flaw. Since the middle of the fourteenth century, we Seares have been marked by a strong aversion to physical activity and a distaste for the jagged realities of life that have drawn us to the sanctuary of universities and libraries. Like other families, we have had our culls, our intellectual runts who lacked those skills of cadging the obscure and re-phrasing the obvious that distinguish the successful scholar. For these "Lesser Seares" there has always been the Church, in which shelter from both doubt and knowledge they have flourished. The tales and fragments that constitute this physically (and metaphorically) thin volume were set to parchment some six hundred years ago by the first and the least of us.

Over the centuries it has been our custom to initiate each son into responsible manhood by acquainting him with our Family Secret, which ritual of passage is performed upon the occasion of his intellectual puberty: his first academic publication. It must be understood straight off that the Family Secret is in no way a family pride; rather, it is a blot and a shame of the kind that binds families together in a spirit of mutual defence.

This secret shame is in the form of a manuscript written by a distant ancestor, Davydd ap Seare. Although much in these tales would be of interest to students of the customs and mores of the fourteenth century, we Seares have been so unscholarly as to hide them from public scrutiny, fearing the effect upon our reputations as much as the effects on the earthier instincts of young readers. Indeed, the two Seares whose lives spanned that era of moral constriction to which Queen Victoria gave her name (and much of her flair) came close to burning the scabrous manuscript to prevent it from ever being inflicted on the delicate sensibilities of the uninitiated, offending all that was good in them, and inflaming all that was evil. Even my own father, although a thorough Edwardian and a man of exceptionally healthy conscience, if scullery rumours are to be credited, paled at the thought of making public tales of so saline a tone.

Allow me to describe these tales here and now, so that the more sensitive reader may toss this book aside and avoid arousing his imagination and, perhaps, disgust. The manuscript that is our secret and our shame is a retelling of certain of the Arthurian legends dealing with valour at arms and brave deeds bravely done—hence, "glorious." The language is lusty and scatological beyond the limits of good taste —hence, "rude." And it is more the salty character of the language than the frank sexual content of the stories that exposes them to moral censorship.

Without seeking to defend my ancestor, I would remind the reader that Davydd ap Seare was a product of his time, a man who lived close to the biological core of existence. Plague and famine were ever in the offing, and men lived within sight and smell of death and birth—literal death with bodies bloating in roadside ditches, not our modern pantomime of floral tributes and rhyming cards of condolence, and literal birth with groans and gnawed lips and recriminations of lovers and placentae to be disposed of, not our modern masques of name-choosing and layette selection. Passing every hour in the shadow of hunger, thirst, sadness, and fear, people in my ancestor's time robustly embraced food and wine and laughter and fornication. They called things what they were. A gorging was a gorging; men shat shit; and with laughter and grunts did full-bodied men and women give and take of swiving.

For all that young Moderns pride themselves on liberated open-mindedness that takes the forms of cocktail-party vulgarity, half-witty single entendre, and sensual gluttony masquerading as sexual freedom, they are no less victims of social fashion than were the people of my own era, whose romantic discrimination is now labelled—with some justification —as damaging and diminishing inhibition. Modern licence and permissiveness are no less dictated by self-image and the expectations of peers than was the false modesty of my time. We were narrowly bound, which is certainly not good; Moderns are cut adrift, which is not much better.

It is instructive to note that the Great Freedom

from Good Taste that characterizes the modern era is limited to but one of the biological functions, the one that has been snickered over since the invention of sin. The rest of the catalogue of human imperfection remains camouflaged by circumlocution. We still know "eccentrics," we still "spend pennies," we still have "beauty spots." But my ancestor, as full of language as he was of life, would have scoffed at the dandy who nibbled at a cake because he "felt a little peckish," and he would have shaken his head sadly to hear that a lad and a lass had "made love" or "diddled," firm in the conviction that the child would be a pallid and sickly thing, so tentatively was it made.

The modern blend of vulgarity and prudery finds telling expression in the tale of the matron who, upon a footpath, cried out, "Oh, shit! I just stepped in doggy-do!"

I too am both legatee and victim of my own times, and I suspect that I would have followed the cautious way of my ancestors and passed on the Family Secret to my successors unpublished. But chance has closed that option to me. My youth and middle years were spent in the groves of academe, pruning and gleaning where finer and braver minds planted and harvested. I was forever busy, as most unproductive men are, and marriage never seemed to lie along the path I wandered.

There was, I confess, in my youth one magnificently confused spring, filled with the presence of a gently knowledgeable young woman for whom freedom was more important than security. And from this single patch of colour in my comfortable umber life came the gift of a love child who warmed and illuminated my days. His hand small in mine as we walked in the wood . . . his questions, so simple, so unanswerable . . . his bright face in a room dark with books as he stood on one leg at the window, daydreaming . . . sometimes a nuisance, always a delight . . . suddenly taller than I, deep-voiced, and very independent . . .

But . . . he fell from the sky during the Battle of Britain.

Reluctant Icarus.

Well, well . . . so it is that I can say with some confidence that the thread of the Seare family will be snipped after me, for I am over seventy and the only woman in my life is my housekeeper, who is sublimely plain, and who has elevated scolding nigh to a fine art.

Thus, I have no choice but to pass on these tales, recognising that they are more likely to blemish the body of ancient literature than to adorn it. Nor can I claim to have been up to the task of translating the vigourous fourteenth-century language of my ancestor. Often at my desk I have felt the shade of Davydd ap Seare frowning over my shoulder and muttering the opening words of his apology: *I gloppen and grete that lewed peple louen tales olde, for a good tale yll told, in the tellyng is marde. Greet gloryous Godd thrugh grace of hym selvne schelde us ffro suche schamesdede and synfulle werkes!*

Nicholas Seare, Professor Emeritus
The Other Cottage
Bettws-y-Coed
Caernarvonshire
1967

A P O L I G I A

I AM DISTRESSED unto weeping that unlettered men debase ancient tales, for a good story ill told is marred in the telling. Great Glorious God, through His grace, shield us from such shameful and sinful works!

Scrupulously have these tales been cleansed of such errors and lesings as have crept into them through the ignorance of scribes and story-tellers, and through low-minded efforts to entertain at the cost of verity.

These histories are proffered in the heart's-hope that they will serve as examples of brave and honourable deeds to direct the reader in the ways of righteousness, that he might more fully and blessedly live out his brief and bitter term on this disk, and shorten his sojourn in Purgatory.

Lest frivolous men abuse the intent of these tales by seeking only to lighten their hours in the company of such wonderfully wrought amusements, be it known that the erudite clerke who set them down did study to reduce these *artful histories into the vulgar language with but two purposes in mind, these being the instruction of men less learned than he, and the greater glory of God. He trusts that all fair-minded men will dismiss as slander the false rumour that certain knaves have bruited abroad to the effect that the clerke did have a third purpose in mind: id est, the gathering of fame and profit unto himself. Such as gave birth to this defamation and such as spread it are nought but envious churls, scrofulous whoresons, and libellous lickshits ... though they are begged not to take umbrage at being thus described.*

These words set down in the Year of Grace 1372

Davydd ap Seare, Clerke

S T A V E   I

NIGHT AND STORM:

THE TALE-WEAVERS ARRIVE.

inter descended with remorseless fury upon the upland villages of Wales, driven by a wind so furious that snow and freezing rain falling from scudding clouds above Crib y Ddysgyl did not touch the earth before Bettws-y-Coed. So strengthy was the storm that stones were ripped from ffridd walls and cast bounding into the valleys, causing beasts to scamper, children to amaze, and men to blaspheme.

It was widely preached, and sometimes believed, that the puissance of the tempest was God's revenge for the rare gentle spring Wales had enjoyed the year before, as it is just and meet that the cruelest winter should follow the gentlest May, for the fates have decreed that the path of man shall lie midway between the grove of delight and the grott of despair, and the proper hue of man's lot is grey, if not of a uniform somber colour, then compounded of whites and blacks in turn, of fortune and misfortune. To this ineluctable law of destiny there are but two exceptions: the Lucky and the Unlucky.

Among the Unlucky were such travellers as were caught sans harbour upon the road, and the humble cottagers who did huddle about their hearths and curse the ravenous wind that sucked the fire up the chimney before that gift of Prometheus could warm outstretched hands and proffered fuds.

In all that swirling sea of chaos and misery there was but one island of comfort, the sturdy castle of Dolbadarn wherein three vast hearths did consume a forest of logs to light and temper the great hall.

The Baron of Dolbadarn, warrior of generous renown before time and gluttony had sapped his sinews, stood at the narrow casement overlooking the moat. He drew his thick cape of vair more closely about him and experienced that particular sense of well-being that attends warmth and comfort made precious by comparison with the discomfort of others. Thus does God in His wisdom make use of the suffering of even the least of us to enhance, by contrast, His boons to those born to merit His favour. In this wise, all things conduce to the ultimate good, though it be not given to the low-minded to comprehend the ways of Heaven.

But it was not alone the roaring fires in his high-vaulted hall that warmed the old Baron's heart, nor yet the heavy joint that turned in the hearth, its charred fat spitting and hissing into the flames, nor yet the knowledge that he had been blest with a wife of beauty and appetite who bore her forty years with a dignity that halved them, and with a daughter of nineteen summers, lusty and frick, for whose hand and favours many suitors pled. These boons he accounted the meet and proper privileges of any knight born to land and power who had served God with high valour by bashing the Saracen Paynim in the Holy Lands. What particularly pleased the Baron was anticipation of rich and meaty story-telling this night, for the old warrior's greatest delight was in tales well told.

A new clerick had been installed in the chapel, and this night he would dine for the first time in the hall of Dolbadarn. The Baron rubbed his hands together and chuckled as he looked forward to entertaining stories of old cuckolds with young wives, of cunning swains and willing trulls, of bawdy nuns and sly friars—in sum, to the earthy sort of tales the former priest had amused him with late in the wine, and might be telling still, had he not fallen victim to unkind rumours concerning choirboys. He dearly hoped this new priest would be of the useful deep-drinking and story-telling ilk he preferred, though he harboured a niggling dread that he might turn out to be of that dour sort whose every tale has some leaden moral tacked onto the end, or who babbles on, sans end or pity, of saints and martyrs and such spoilsport persons. The good Baron frowned at the prospect of a dull, elevating priest, but he drew comfort from his conviction that the Saviour Christ would never punish a knight of the cross with the scourge of a pious priest. That would be unfair, and the Baron's pure, simple faith refused to admit any suggestion that God might play the part of the unsporting lout.

The evening waned ... and yet the new priest arrived not. The lady of the manor descended, radiant in a gown of red samite, and took her place at table beside their buxom, full-blooded daughter ... but still the guest arrived not. The Baron's stomach growled complaint at being denied its viands, and the Baron growled back, "The joint be brent, an we attend this discourteous churl longer! To table then! And a devil's piss upon him, if he come sniffing about here once the meal's begun!"

The mistress and her daughter did blush and press their lips together and tap them with their fingertips, as was their wont when the Baron's rough tongue betrayed that his wit had been honed in the company of rude and ready fellows. But for all their pretty blushing, they too felt the claws of hunger, sharpened by the heady smell of roasting meat.

No sooner had the Baron seated himself and lifted a rip of meat to his moistening mouth than there came a beating at the great door.

Slamming the meat upon the table with an oath, the Baron rose and strode to the portal with angry pace, muttering sincere imprecations against all such uncivil whoresons as make a practice of banging upon a man's door just when his teeth are atingle with anticipation. A serving man rushed to the door in advance of the master and, throwing it open with a vigour calculated to demonstrate his eagerness to serve, had the misfortune to run the oaken mass over his liege's great toe.

Thus it was that when the priest entered into the hall he was smitten by the piety of the Baron, whom he found kneeling upon the floor, beating his breast and wailing and calling upon God in more forms and usages than were within the priest's ken.

Whilst the Baron was engaged in earnestly supplicating by God's eyes, wounds, beard, and nether parts, the ladies of the hall swept forward to receive their guest with joli courtesies, which civilities they redoubled upon discovering that this man of God lacked those qualities of age and ugliness appropriate to his calling. He was, in fact, marked by youth, manly beauty, golden locks that belied his tonsure, and a body sinewy and well-made in all parts.

They took from him his dripping cape and bade him warm himself at the hearth before partaking of refreshment. The young priest did most courtly-wise and with pretty flow of words make his apologies for late arrival, pleading the rigours of weather and his ignorance of the way, as he had not before been guest to the manor nor had the privilege of the company of its beautiful and gracious ornaments. Blushing and pushing at his chest with their fingers, the ladies bade him leave off excuses, so heart-glad were they that he had found his way at last. And the daughter proffered the hope that he should come to know the way well in future, for she would fain have him no stranger to their home, and she begged him to make free with whatsoever he found to his liking.

With such dulcet and flattering speech, the ladies did guide the young priest to the well-provisioned table and make a place for him betwixt them. The good Baron hobbled to the table, where he did seek to entertain his guest, asking how it came to pass that so fair and strapping a lad had been doomed to the priesthood, which calling was commonly the resort of dim and feeble sons who had escaped being women by only a matter of inches and often, it was rumoured, by no more than an inch . . . though no offence was intended.

The priest lowered his eyes and recounted modestly the custom in his family to offer up to the church the wisest of their sons, the strengthiest, and the most fair, thus losing three sons to God in each generation, until his own, in which they were required to sacrifice but one.

The daughter avowed it a very pretty and pious custom indeed, and one that might with honour be followed by other clans, which seemed content to sacrifice to God only the lees and dregs, the runts of the litter, as it were. And beneath the table she touched the young man's hand and, finding it still afrost, placed it into the warmth of her lap as a gesture of love for all God's creatures. The young man smiled upon her with gentle grace, accepting the kindness in the spirit in which it was given.

"Well, then," declared the Baron, "to meat! And famine take the hindmost! And after you've had your gorge, wight priest, we shall try whether thou hast sleight of tongue in story-telling to lighten the evening hours." So saying, the old knight lifted a dripping morsel with his fingers and was on the instant of letting it plop into his upturned mouth when there came an eerie scritching at the great door.

"What now?" roared the Baron, flinging his meat across the room in fury. He rose with a snarl and hobbled across the hall to the door, where he was met by the servant. "An thou openest that door upon my toe again," promised the Baron, "the dogs will break their fast upon thine arse!"

Cringing and muttering apologies, the serving man slid open a spyhole artfully emplaced in the great door, whereunto he did set his eye and peer out into the dark and storm.

"Well, man?" demanded the Baron. "What is it that scritches thus eerily upon the door?"

The servant closed the spyhole and wiped the rain from his eye. "Tis a hag, your lordship."

"A hag? A hag? What sort of hag, for the love of Jesu?"

Again the servant set his eye to the hole. "Well, sire, I would describe her as your ordinary run of hags, such as might be seen begging in the market-place of any small to middling town. Tis a hag whose face is confected for the most part of wrinkles and furrows, whose nose is a bony hook, whose eyes are beady and sunken, and whose thin-lipped mouth might be said to be innocent of teeth, were it not for one fang that dangles from the center top."

"Here, let me see!" The Baron pushed the serving man aside and set his own eye to the spyhole. "Aye, thou hast the right of it. Tis a hag, to be sure. But thou hast omitted to mention that her pate is bald, save for a dizaine of hairs that dangle wetly into her face. Nor didst thou note the black whisker that sprouts from the wart decorating her nose."

The servant begged leave to peer again through the hole, where he did close one eye and bulge the other. "Truly, sire, I did overlook those adjuncts to her ugliness. But even you, master, have failed to limn the long and bony frame revealed by the clinging of her sodden garment and unrelieved by the usual upper ornaments of womanhood—lest those be they, those limp entrails that dangle listlessly to her belly."

"Be not forward, base person! I had noted those graces thou describest, but I wot them to merit no mention, as they fall within every man's vision of a hag, and are therefore said unsaid. But enough of this entertainment! To table!" And so saying, the Baron betook himself to the feasting boards, where he found the sturdy priest in close and civil parlance with the ladies. "Come, young man!" commanded the Baron. "Leave off these unmanly niceties and tuck in! Nor abuse a good gorging with the womanly affectations lately introduced from France. I do not hold with such pingling dainties as the sucking off of the fingers betwixt rips of meat. Come, man! Fall to with vigour! And for God's sake, use both hands!"

"Nay, Father," said the daughter, squirming and quetching. "The good priest has no need to use both hands, as he does wonderously well and skilfully with but one."

Seeking to delight his senses with the teasing of them, the Baron eyed his meat long and longingly, sniffing of its savour and clicking his teeth together in anticipation of the excellent work before them. With luxurious slowness, he raised the morsel to his moistening mouth and . . .

But again came the scritching at the door, somewhat more insistent than before.

The Baron was wood wroth as he sent wine cups and serving platters crashing against the walls and kicked dogs yelping to the corners of the great hall. "What in God's name is it now!" he thundered.

Cringing, the serving man begged leave to opine that it might be the hag, still begging entrance to the hall and shelter from the cruel elements.

"What? What!" cried the Baron. "What need have I for a hag? What caitifhede is this? Does she consider no one's feelings but her own? Take some hearty lads to the parapet and drop a stone or two upon her head for a nuisance! Snatch up the drawbridge and mash her against the door like a fly swatted upon the table with a neighbor's joint of meat! Wring her head from her scraggy neck and cram it up her cul, that she have a lesson in manners! Grasp her brittle legs and pull them apart, first making a wish! In these and other ways of your own contrivance, teach the bitch manners, ere I lose my temper!"

The Baron returned to table and begged his guest's pardon for these interruptions, declaring them enough to ruin a man's appetite. But the priest parlayed in behalf of the hag, saying that God's commandments behoove us to care for even the least of His flock. By argument and sleight of logick, the priest did persuade towards the recreation of the hag, that there might be something to attract the Baron's notice, lest he ken what he had privily in hand.

Grudgingly, the Baron commanded that the hag be granted entrance and permitted to cower in a distant corner of the hall. Then it occurred to him that the priest, being lately arrived in the village and perhaps not cognizant of the Baron's repute for kindliness, might not know him to be as Christian as the next man—or priest—so he further ordered that the hag be given a pot of gruel to allay her hunger and a stout stick to keep the dogs at bay.

These acts of charity done, the Baron betook himself again to table, where, with mistrustful eye upon the door, he did thrice make pretence as though he would eat, hoping to foil ironic fortune that seemed bent upon interrupting his feasting. Finding these baits untaken, he perceived himself free at last to wage fine combat amongst the viands, and did therefore take up his meat and offer to set his teeth thereinto.

But his wife grasped his arm in the very action of biting, and the morsel slapped his eye right smartly.

"Hush!" said the wife, her voice strangled with fright. "Hearest thou that?"

"Hear I what?" demanded the Baron, grinding his teeth and keeping but slack rein on his temper.

"It meseemeth I heard a moaning beyond the great door."

"Tis but the wind, good wife. Think no more on't, and grant me leave to gorge."

"But nay!" insisted the wife, grasping his arm again and setting the meat to his ear. "Tis other than the wind I hear. Tis a right mournful sound such as maidens make at the moment of completion."

"An thou quitest not thy grip upon my arm, good wife, thou shalt surely have this joint across thy fair and beauteous face," promised the Baron.

"Nay, husband, nay! Let not thy manly wrath becloud thy reason. Do but try the truth of my fears and thou shalt know I mistake me not. Prithee, be not a churlish lout in this, nor yet a brainless ass, as I would not have our guest mistake thee for a misbegotten whoreson and a brutish shit." So gently and with such tones of loving grace did the wife say this that the Baron relented and consented to her wish, and for the third time that night did he open the great oaken door and peer out against the wind-harried rain.

"What's this? Some low knave from the village hath made bold to leave on our threshold a pile of filthy rags the stench of which is wonderous noxious, though it be mixt with this brisk wind that doth chill me to the very marrow and make me wish with all my soul that this door before me were closed."

"Art thou sure it be nought but a filthy and reeking pile of rags?" called out the wife. "For still do I hear an unearthly moaning."

"Ah, as to that, fair wife, the mystery is quickly solved. Tis this heap of scrofulous rags that does moan from time to time, each moaning accompanied by a feeble movement thereof." So saying, the Baron closed the great door and yode him to the wide hearth, where to the fire he did proffer first his hands then his fud, that some of the chill might be drawn therefrom.

"Pray leave off the unseemly rubbing of thine arse, husband," begged the mistress, "and give over thy bootless ramblings about the hall, lest our guest mistake thine absence from table for a gesture of inhospitality. For now that the feasting be nearly done, we should take a cup of wine and pray the good priest to entertain us with pious and illuminating tales."

"What?" the Baron cried. "Call you the feasting nearly done when I have yet to set tooth to meat? Where's the justice in that?" Yet he drew some consolation from the anticipation of entertainment, for next to wine and food, he took greatest delight in stories of low adventure and high valour, in rude tales and glorious. Most of all did he love tales that made him laugh, particularly those of cuckolded husbands, whom he held in deepest ridicule, and stories of maidens foined deep and well before the very eyes of befuddled fathers, whom he also held in scorn.

"Aye," said the Baron. "Do let us have a tale or two, lest this evening come to no account at all. But thou, my daughter, hadst best betake thee to thy chamber, not alone because I hope the stories will be of meat and matter unfit for maiden ears, but also because I ween thou art ill and on the veriest verge of some dire malady, for oft and again has the blood come to thy cheeks and thy breath come in gasps, and I did hear thee moan low upon two occasions."

As the priest quickly withdrew his hand from her lap, the daughter pled, "Nay, father, banish me not above! Gramercy for thy kind solicitude, but thou dost err to think me ill. The colour that mounted to my cheeks was but the blush of maidenhood when I bethought me that the beef turning on yon spit, all unclothed, might in life have been a male. The gasping and panting did but derive from the pity I felt for yon misfortunate, ugly, low, loathsom, and scurvy hag, who, though she be vile and disgusting, is no less one of God's creatures and deserving of our concern. As to the moaning . . . ah . . . ah . . . it issued not from me, but rather from the pile of reeking rags you yourself did discover beyond the great door. And when, in pretty fatherly care, thou fearest lest the stories of this priest might be unfit for maiden ears, thou dost the pious man injustice, for I trust he knows none but saintly and instructive tales." And with this she smiled upon the young clerick, took his hand, and replaced it into her lap.

"Dreadest thou so?" mused the aged knight with a frown. "I fear thou mayest have the right of it, and his tales be naught but arid and moral-laden. Tell me, lad, what stories have ye conned for the amusement of such noble lords as offer you feasting, though they themselves have scarce found time to shove a morsel down their own gullets?"

The handsome clerick smiled modestly upon the ladies as he averred that, although he claimed no great sleight in the telling of tales, he had indeed rehearsed a story or two that he hoped they might not find totally lacking in merit. "Wouldst thou, sire, be informed of the dire, glorious, and right sad death and martyrdom of Saint Sebastian?"

The Baron's face fell. "O, that one. The fellow with all the arrows sticking out of him, and his eyes upturned as though to admonish a bird that had shat upon his pate. With all courtesy, good priest, I confess that I like not that tale. Threescore times have I heard it, and still I fail to see the humour in it." The Baron's expression took on a look of sly connivance as he pushed the priest's arm with his elbow. "Come, lad, couldst thou not instead weave a tale of a burgher's wife who put horns on the old fool by sporting with an apprentice? A fair lesson it would be for us to know the ungodly ways of townsfolk, and we would study to avoid their errors and save our souls."

"Truly, I know no such histories, my good lord."

"Shit," muttered the Baron earnestly.

"But if thou wouldst, I might regale thee with

telling of the ecstasy some saints have known when the spirit of God entered within them."

"Oh, do!" cried the daughter. "Do let us hear of ecstasies!"

"Nay, nay," grumbled the Baron. "If your lore be limited to the doings of saints, at least let us hear of such as Saint Michael. Now there was a joli saint! And a knight to boot, which is more than thy Saint Sebastian can claim, he who lacked the good sense to hide behind a tree when they were shooting arrows at him. Damned fool! . . . though I say it with no disrespect. Tell us, I prithee, of how Saint Michael grappled with the foul dragon. Describe how that fire-belching beast was wont to take off maidens and have his way with them, and feel free to limn these doings with close detail. Then, look ye, picture for us the good knight's combat, and how he did chop off the monster's manhood and club him with it! That's a good bit! Then recount how the knight did reach down the beast's throat and grasp his tail and with a whip of his mighty arm did snap the dragon inside out that he might kick his fud from within!" The Baron's eyes glowed as he drew his chair close to the priest's and rubbed his hands together. "Aye, aye. Tell us of such uplifting things as these!"

"Truly, sire," protested the clerk, "although I am well acquainted with the tale of Saint Michael, I wot not such incidents as you describe."

The old knight frowned. "But I got the tale from the old priest that had the living before you. A goodly man," added the Baron, cocking a meaningful eye at the priest, "and one who knew how to spin a lively tale to earn his found and fodder, which is more than

can be said for some, if you catch the subtle drift of
my meaning there."

The wily priest bethought himself to veer the par-
lay away from himself and towards other matters. "Ah
... there is a wonderment that has troubled me for
some small time, sire."

"Aye? And what be that?" asked the Baron.

"I am but newly familiar with these parts—"

"Why dost thou snicker, daughter?" demanded
the Baron. "Pray, do not show bad breeding by interrupting the good man when he may be on the verge
of telling us something entertaining."

"Seems it not strange to you," the priest continued, "that a pile of rags, however filthy and reeking,
would have the power to moan and move?"

The Baron pondered this, his brow furrowed with
the effort. "Hm-m-m. Now I think on't, tis somewhat
odd. What make you of it?"

"Truly, sire, I know not what interpretation to
place upon the thing, save it be a sign from heaven
commanding you ever to persist in your hospitality to
His anointed servants."

"The Miracle of the Rags?" asked the Baron, his
voice aweful.

"O, as to it being a miracle, sire, I could not make
so bold as to attest to that. For, mark ye," the priest
said, his voice low and hollow, "there be other forces
than those of heaven abroad on a stormy night."

"How?" cried the mistress of the manor. "Thinkest thou this might be the work of the devil?" In her
fright she grasped the young man's free hand and
clutched it to her breast.

Thus delightfully crucified, the clerick pursued,

"With no more evidence than now in hand, I dare not claim the one or the other."

The Baron rose. "I'll put an end to this speculation, by God! I shall test the pile of rags. If it be a God-sent miracle, I shall do prayer and obeyance. If it be an incubus of the devil disguised as a heap of mouldering rags, I'll kick its fud down the road. One way or the other, I must be satisfied!"

"And so must I," cried the daughter.

"And so must I," cried the wife.

Steeling himself to face again the angry elements, the old knight crossed the hall and flung open the great door. The reek of the rags drove him back several paces, but, summoning his courage, he advanced and prodded the heap with his sword. It stirred and moaned.

In her fright, the mistress kneaded the priest's hand against her breasts.

Again and again the knight prodded the pile of stenchy rags with his sword, each prod rewarded by movements that grew to palpable twitchings and squirms as the moans grew into cries and yelps. At last, the Baron made so bold as to catch a bit of rag upon the point of his sword and lift it that he might peek beneath. . .

His laughter filled the hall.

"'Tis neither angel nor demon after all!" he cried. "'Tis but a scrawny and disgusting beggar who seems to have small wounds all about his body—marks of some dread disease, I doubt me not." And with that, he closed the great door and returned into the room, laughing heartily at their mistaking a humble clapperdudgeon for the agent of God. "That's a good one on us!" he declared.

"But are you not going to grant him harbour from the storm?" asked the priest, remembering his Christian duty maugre considerable drains on his attention.

"Is it not enough that I have fouled our chambers with yonder hag?" asked the Baron. "If I drag in this reeking sack of bones, I fear the dogs may bite him and fall ill." But seeing that both his wife and daughter did squirm with anguishes of pity for the poor creature, the knight relented. "O, very well! Have the whoreson in! But he must leave his festering rags without, for the stench of them doth make mine eyes to burn." And he directed his servants to take up tongs and strip the beggar naked before chucking him into a corner of the hall, but they were cautioned to select a corner well away from that in which the hag grovelled, lest these unclean two fall upon one another in dismal lust; for it was the Baron's belief that from the mating of such as these did derive those dreadful grotesques that peer down from the eaves of cathedrals.

Upon returning to table, the Baron sighed and shook his head. "Tis a great pity, young priest, that our festivities are diminished by your want of stories with which to regale us. But perchance all is not lost. Though thou art dully void of lusty tales of combat in the lists and on the lits, and I would gag to hear such dour tales of saintliness as thou kennest, yet might we find pretty compromise in the oft-told tales of ancient Arthur and his Knights of the Table Round. True, these tales have been spoke and heard again and again, till they are beyond surprise and wonder, yet they be worn so smooth with the telling and retelling of them that they do sometimes slip through the memory. So it is that, for all their sere and hoary age, they will serve when nothing better there is."

"Good sire," replied the priest, "I would not deny thine urging, but tristly I know not the tales of which thou speakest. But I promise to study to improve myself in this particular, for it is my strongest desire to satisfy each and every member of this noble family."

The mistress of the manor squeezed his hand, and through it her bubbie, and she giggled. And the daughter smiled behind her hand.

"What's this?" demanded the Baron. "Is there some amusement abroad that has escaped my ken? Why gigglest thou, wife? Wherefore smilest thou, daughter? And thou, priest! Whence these winks and snickers? Is everyone to be entertained but me? Where's the justice in that, pray tell?"

"Nay, nay, good husband," said the wife. "Thou art amiss to assume that we share any jest and keep it from thee." But she laughed aloud, though she sought to suppress it. And the daughter stretched her face bland, though her eyes sparkled with merriment.

The Baron frowned deeply. "I'll not have amusement in my hall, lest I be a part of it, do you hear! I must know the spring and source of all these giggles and smiles and winks and snickers! Well, priest? Come, come! Out with it!"

But as the priest fumbled for words, a loud and inhuman moan filled the great hall.

"What in the name of God's Groin was *that?*" demanded the old knight.

The serving man came forward and said, "Tis the naked wretch you lately gave comfort and shelter to, sire, that dares to moan and grede so discourteously."

"But why? Are the dogs at his leg?"

"Nay, sire. There's not meat enough there to command their interest."

"Then require the shitten whoreson to leave off his damned moaning! And to inspire him to take the advice to heart, take up something large and bash him smartly and often."

The servants did as their master bade, and for some duration they plied the old beggar's back and head with such staffs and bits of ironmongery as came easily to hand. But this instruction seemed more to increase than diminish his complaints.

"Devil take the bony bastard!" the Baron raged. "This is what comes of bringing such rubbish from the storm and granting it the hospitality of our home! Give them an inch and they'll take an ell, and that's the truth. Drag the ungrateful clapperdudgeon before me that he may answer to my wrath!"

"But sire," remonstrated the servant, "is it proper to bring the scroff into the presence of ladies, bare of arse and pissette as he is?"

"Thou hast a delicate sensibility for one of your low quality. It would indeed be discourteous to drag him up in all his wretched nakedness, particularly as the ladies have but recently done with eating. Tell you what. Clap a cheese rind over his dangling bits and tie it off behind. As for his arse, require him on pain of beating to stand so as to direct it away from the ladies' scrutiny."

All was done as the Baron ordered, and in a short

time the emaciated old beggar stood before the table, quivering with cold and all naked save for his cheese rind. Full ugly the wretch was, a vision to make strong wenches miscarry, and in no wise had his appearance been improved by the probing of the Baron's sword, nor by the attentions of the servants with their sticks and bits of ironmongery. The ladies did gag and turn their faces away, and one old dog howled and fell swooning upon the reeds.

"How's this!" cried the Baron. "Dare you still to moan, thou impudent glob of whore's spittle?"

The beggar raised his sunken eyes to the knight and opened his mouth as though to speak, displaying teeth as nicely castellated as any manor wall. But no speech issued forth, but rather a sound compounded of sobbing, moaning, and whimpering.

"Speak up, you festering pile of ratshit," the Baron urged.

At last, with trembling effort, the beggar managed to utter, "Aye, me."

"Aye, me?" asked the Baron. "After all this disturbance, all you can say for yourself is: 'Aye, me'? You'd best do better than that, an you would keep bowels and brawn in the same county!"

Summoning forth all his strength, the old beggar croaked, "'Tis the irony of it, good my lord."

"Of what irony croakest thou?"

Great tears dripped from the dim and sunken eyes as the beggar said, "To think that these ladies turn their faces from me in disgust, where once every maiden in England did smile upon me and beg that I carry her favour into single combat!"

"Thou?" questioned the Baron. "In single combat? With what? A flea?"

The ancient wretch groaned and continued. "Ah, what bitter fate to find myself cast into the corner of a hall, where once I held sway over seven times seven castles, the least of which would not use this place to house the servants' privy."

"Privy? Privy!"

"To think that I starve, with not a crust to keep my belly from my spine, where once I commanded such feastings as would make these viands, by comparison, nought but what I threw to the lesser of my dogs."

In taut silence the Baron leaned forward, his eyes bulging. Then he said in a level voice, "Enjoy this speech of thine richly, foul scroff, for surely it will be thy last."

But the beggar ignored this sage advice. "For years have I born my misery with good grace and without complaint, but this evening, hearing you speak of good King Arthur and his worthy knights, my heart did crack and perhaps some small moan did escape my lips."

"Mad bobaunce!" declared the Baron. Then he smiled and winked at his fellow diners. "And tell me, whimpering wad of slime, of what quality dost thou fancy thyself to be, that by contrast all that I am and possess are so low and scornworthy?" And he nudged the priest with his elbow and bloated out his cheeks.

Then bravely did the beggar thrust out his narrow chest

And manfully did lift his face to family and guest
He squared his scrawny shoulders and tightened his
*   behind*
And cleared his throat, and took a breath, and set
*   aright his rind*
And out spake he with fervour no man would dare
*   to mock*
"I am he . . .
*   that once was styled . . .*
*   Sir Launcelot du Lac!"*

At first astonished silence froze the tongues of all that host. How could this ragged scroff before them verify his boast? They turned to one another; unbelieving eyes did blink to hear this blasphemy from one composed of stench and stink. The silence then was shattered as the diners one and all brast forth in peals of laughter that rebounded through the hall.

Full richly did the company roar with merriment at the claim of this scarecrow shivering before them to be the one and veriest Launcelot du Lac, fairest ornament of British chivalry. And the Baron jeered, saying, "What wood bobaunce is this? An thou hadst claimed to be the weapon, rather than the knight, I might have believed thee; for truly thy scant frame has more the shape of a lance than a Launcelot!"

Yet with solemn dignity did the beggar maintain his claim to noble station, and he did remonstrate against the Baron in sad voice, saying that this unkind railing did ill become a brother knight.

"An thou wert my brother, shrunk clapperdudgeon, I must believe my sainted mother had made

"I AM HE . . .

THAT ONCE WAS STYLED . . .

SIR LAUNCELOT DU LAC!"

the beast with two backs against grim Famine himself!"

Then the mistress touched her husband's sleeve and whispered aside to the effect that there might be some joli merriment to be had in setting this reeking beggar to a trial of questions, to try how he might defend his pretext. Thus it was that the Baron did smooth his grinning face with his palm into a countenance of gravity and did say unto the naked beggar, "Tell me, good knight, how came you to be wandering the earth and moaning at good men's doors in this age? For if I mistake me not the days of King Arthur are past these six hundred years."

"Ah, my brother knight," the beggar intoned, "it is as you doubtless suspect. A tale of enchantment and evil influence lies behind my endless wanderings."

"A tale?" The Baron's face glowed with alerted interest. "A tale, sayest thou? Hast thou a tale of enchantment and evil about thee? Pray offer it forth, for fain would I have a tale to amuse me."

"Eagerly, good brother, would I share my history with thee—a history which touches here and there upon low adventures of lust and cunning—but, alack, I cannot."

"What lets thee, man, for God's sake?" asked the Baron.

"I lack the strength, cousin, having nought eaten these six days but herbs and grass and such marrow bones as I could wrench from the jaws of inhospitable dogs. And yet, for all my dire weakness, I would essay to grant thy wishes, were I not confused and confounded with embarrassment to appear before you and these beauteous ladies with nought but a cheese rind twixt my manhood and their eyes, and nought upon mine arse but draughts. For know you that the very word, 'embarrassment,' was coined to describe the condition of one who stands 'bare-assed.' " So saying, he did bow and make a gracious sweep of his arm.

"Truly," quoth the wife, "yon Sir Blight doth speak right cunningly and with courteous words beyond his seeming station in life."

"Be on guard, madam," interposed the priest. "These pretty speeches do not alone confer nobility upon Sir Plague. For know ye that wandering bards and minstrels do practise to speak artfully and with grace, though they be nought but artists, and therefore lower than the meanest villein."

"And yet," spake out the Baron, "if yon Sir Scab has indeed lusty tales and rude in him, even as despised minstrels do, then it would profit us to throw some discarded raiment about his bones and place before him a bowl of scraps and fat, that we might have the telling of them to ease our evening." He ordered his servants to see this done, and in less time than the telling, the beggar-knight had a vast, if shitten, cape about him and was waging mighty destruction in a basin of orts and fat still tepid from the feast. So vigourously did he set to his work, and with such slurpings and gulpings, that the others did have to lift their voices to be heard.

"Think you, priest," shouted the Baron, "that there might be some truth in this story of enchantment and bewitching? For such things do happen, I wot. And I note that the fellow does eat with a force and authority I have seen amongst knights of the highest order."

The handsome clerick scoffed and poohed and declared that in all his holy training he had not encountered a true and verified story of enchantment.

"Nay, proud priest, be not quick to dismiss such things. I intend no offence to your feeble calling when I say that priests do not know everything, although they think themselves in lore above the common because they practice at the marring of sheepskins with ink and pretend these scribblings are words every bit as good as those a man might speak out from his mouth. If yon slurping fellow be a knight suffering under dire enchantment, then I, a warrior knight, would be more like to recognise him than would any soft clerick whose vows do preclude him from wielding even that most catholic weapon of all."

"But, good host, our Lord and Saviour hath in His wisdom made His priests to be the instruments of His truth and infinite knowledge."

"As for that, young fellow, know you that the good Lord Christ, perfect though He be, was not Himself a fighting man, and little kenned the ways of warriors and knights. I say this with all humility, of course, and in the knowledge that He doth eavesdrop on our every word."

The priest frowned deeply. "I trust that what I hear is not the seed of that vile weed heresy."

"Not a bit of it! In all things that are God's—life and death, Heaven and Hell, plague and pestilence, perdition and purgatory—I humbly account myself the lowest of His servants (although there be many lower than I, and I could name some, an I would). But Lord Jesu was a man of peace and love, and war was not His calling. He hath done things that would blush

a true and belted knight, though I blame Him not for
it, as He was nought but the son of a carpenter and
lacked the good fortune to be prenticed out a squire
and learn the ways of manhood."

At this the priest did squirm uncomfortably, cast-
ing looks of dread towards the ceiling. "Ah . . . and in
what ways dost thou maintain that Lord Jesu acted
unmanfully, pray tell?"

"O, oft and again did He so! Consider only His
last days and rare irksome passion. Now, had it been
I those whoresons Romans made to drag that cross
about the streets, and had they made so bold as to
scorn *me* with the clapping onto my head of a crown
of thorns, I would have laid about me with that mighty
forked club till it did dire work amongst those jeering
Roman bastards, and a full score of them would have
had their heads broken for their instruction, and the
captain amongst them would have walked in rare risible manner, what with that crown of thorns stuffed
up his cul!"

"But, mine host—"

"O, I know, I know. Such were not the ways of
gentle Jesu. Doubtless there was high cunning behind His seeming cowardice, for in the end His faith
did conquer and drive the Roman whoresons down to
Hell. O, yes, I admit God to be a clever and vengeful
fellow in His own way, and I full admire Him for it. I
say only that He chose to *feign* the part of a snivelling,
cringing lickspittle, the better to attack from the cover
of kindness. I attach no blame to such craft and cunning. But truth is truth, and it must be said. Take you,
for fair example, that moment when the Saviour was
hanging on the cross and crying out from very thirst,

and those lickshit Romans did have sport with him by the setting of vinegar to His lips. I warrant ye, lad, had it been *me* dangling from the rood, and had they had the effrontery to proffer *me* bitter vinegar, I would have climbed down and done such mighty work with the toe of my boot that I would have driven their crotches to their Adam's apples, and all the world would have marvelled at the wonderous length of their strides!"

"I fear I do lose the point of all this, my lord," confessed the priest uneasily.

"My burden be but this. It is I, and not you, who would be most like to know if yon loudly gulping and gorging beggar is a true and belted knight."

At this moment the daughter of the house suddenly stood and cried out, swaying in her misery, the back of her hand clapped to her alabaster brow.

"How now?" cried the Baron in deep concern. "Why dost thou grede and quetch so?"

"Truly, Father, all this talk of the Saviour hath made me bethink myself of my sins, for which I am woefully regretful. I do dread to carry the damning fardle of them upon my soul for another moment!"

"Said like a good and Christian child," shouted the Baron. "But what haste? Thou art in good health and strengthy, and death be not like to catch thee up this night. Surely thou bearest upon thy sweet soul none but the slightest smears, like the nibbling of a sweetmeat in Lent, or some trivial lapse in the honouring of thy mother."

"Nay, Father," shouted the girl, "all sins, even such modest and graceful ones as I do carry upon my maiden soul, are loathsom and foul in His sight. I must have this young priest confess me forthwith and free me from my distress."

"But daughter, whilst thou be above in thy chambers being shriven by this fellow, thou shalt surely miss some part of good Sir Launcelot's tale, which I have no doubt he will get to, once he is done with that *goddamned deafening slurping!* Can't you leave off for a moment, for the love of Christ?"

But the daughter persisted, tilting her pleading face this way and that until the doting father relented. "Well, an thou must have it so. In truth, I confess it pleases me some to have so Christian a daughter as doth place her inner needs foremost. Go you, priest, with her to her chambers, and see that you shrive her to her deepest satisfaction."

The clerick promised to do so with all vigour and dispatch.

As the two withdrew towards the thither chambers, the old knight turned to his wife and asked, "Why scowlest thou so? Why be thy brow drawn up in such a semblance of concern and distress? Prithee, dwell not upon our daughter's slight sins, but instead picture the promised vigour and rare force with which the priest will soon shrive her. Now, leave off the gnawing of thy fingers and the slapping of thy brow, whilst this good beggar-knight abandons his slurping and gorging for a time to share with us fine tales of Arthur and his knights. On with the stories, brother knight!"

At this, the whilom beggar, now knight, made haste to finish off the last morsel of fat, then did he lick the sides and bottom of the basin with such good will that it wanted not washing for two years thereafter, then he sat back and released a belch that fluttered the most distant flambeaux.

"So kindly hast thou feasted me," quoth he, "that I am prete to amuse and amaze thee with tales till the dawn be blushing the eastward hills."

The Baron grinned and rubbed his palms together. "Ah, good! Fine! And which of the tales of good King Arthur wilt thou give us first? Will it be the adventures of steady Sir Gawain? Or those of the delicate Sir Gay? Or those of rustic Persival? Or handsome Galahad? Pray, commence where thou wouldst and prepare for a long siege of talking, for I vow I am mooded to hear tales all this night through. And, should thy mind run dry of tales of valour, of arms and the man, I would not be irked shouldst thou eke out the evening with some light stories of millers' wives disporting themselves with apprentices in a hogshead."

"Truly, fellow knight," said the antique beggar, "I must study where to begin, so many and fine are the tales that teem within my memory. Perhaps if I had a sip of wine to wet my throat, the words would more freely flow."

And the Baron bade the servants fill the cup of the beggar, but that worthy did instead offer out the basin to be brimmed up, and when it was so, did drain off full half of it without a rest.

All this while, the hag in her corner did watch these happenings with great interest and something akin to envy. And when she saw half a basin of wine disappear down the beggar's throat, she did swallow with him in sympathy, and did even wipe her lips with her shitten sleeve and essay to belch, as though

it had been down her own dusty gorge the full red
wine had coursed.

"What say ye," spake out the beggar-knight, "to
beginning at the very beginning, and hearing from me
the true and little-known story of how Arthur did become King through plucking out the sword from the
heart of stone?"

"How? Claimest thou this to be a story little
known?" asked the Baron, "Why, that tale is known
by every babe that dangles from its mother's teat."

"Ah, good sire, you mistake to believe that the
true tale be known to every babe that pukes on its
mother's chest."

"Dost claim it is false, the tale known to every
babe that shits yellow into its mother's palm?"

"False it is, I assure you. False as the vows of a
lusty nun. False as the promises of a stiffened lover.
False as the intent of the wife who waves farewell
to her crusading husband, while there lurks in the
cupboard a locksmith to have at the chastity belt. False
as—"

"Say false and be done with it!"

"False, then! I alone know the true telling of the
event, confessed to me by Arthur himself one night
when he was in his cups."

"Ah! Then by all means let us have it."

"At last!" cried the mistress.

"Yea, wife, I confess it takes some doing, the
dragging forth of a tale from the mouth of this—" But
the Baron saw he had mistaken his wife's meaning
when he followed her hard gaze and espied his
daughter and the young priest returning from her
chambers. Right fully had the girl confessed herself,

for there was a blush of joy on her fair visage and a swimming gentleness in her eye that was certain sign of that happiness that comes of being truly purged. The priest, by contrast, showed marks of fatigue and strain, so vigourously had he applied himself to the shriving of her, for the Baron did note that the good clerick had mortified his flesh on her behalf, for there were scratches upon the nape of his neck and small blue bruises upon his throat. Verily, it seemed as though the priest, in releasing her of the burden of her sins, had taken their weight upon himself, for she did younger seem and more buoyant than before, whilst he did appear older and more drawn, and indeed he did walk somewhat gingerly.

"Come, sit, good priest," said the Baron, "and tell me, now that thou knowest the inmost secrets of my fair daughter, is not her breeding wonderous fine?"

The priest did confess that her breeding was amongst the best and tightest he had known.

"Think not that I study to snare compliments, good priest," said the Baron, "but have I not a daughter well taught and well reared?"

"I did find her right roundly reared," averred the priest. "And indeed the strength of her rearing did lighten my task wonderfully."

Whilst the Baron and the priest conversed in this wise, the mistress of the manor whispered into her daughter's ear, and the maiden startled and hastened to tuck back into her bodice a finely formed bubbie that had flopped adrift in the vigour of the shriving, which action she performed with coy and bashful blushes that affirmed her fine modesty.

The Baron turned to his daughter and beamed.

"By good chance, you arrive back just in season to hear the only true and little-known tale of the Sword and the Stone, sweet girl. Pray you, Sir Launcelot, begin your history!"

Then Launcelot did hush the room and in sonorous
   tone
Did undertake to share the tale of Arthur, Sword,
   and Stone.

S T A V E   II

IN WHICH SIR LAUNCELOT RECOUNTS THE FALL

OF ANCIENT TROY AND THE EXPLOITS OF SIR

ACHILLES AND SIR HECTOR, TOGETHER WITH

A FULL ACCOUNTING OF THEIR TRIST

DEATHS, AND SUNDRY DETAILS OF

THE SACKING OF TROY.

ut hold!" the Baron bellowed, his
  voice in manly rage,
As in each hand he grasped a word
  to lean out from the page
And squint up to scan the lines that
heralded the Stave.
"Wouldst play me false, Sir Launcelot? Wouldst act
 the part of knave?
Thou promised tales of Arthur's knights. What
 bodes this scurvy ploy?
Dost thou forsake the Table Round and choose the
 Fall of Troy?"

Sir Launcelot answered, saying, "Surely thou knowest that the path to the Sword and the Stone begins in antique Troy. Every fool knows that!"

"Dost?" asked the Baron, eyeing Launcelot mistrustfully.

"Dost. Or at least I shall weave it so. The night be yet young and the storm still rages, and I would have my tales endure through this miserable season. At all events, fellow knight, it be I who spin these tales, and if thou likest not my ways of doing it, then a devil's fart engulf thee!"

The Baron spake behind his hand to the priest. "Note ye? He proves himself a true knight after all. Who but one familiar with the usages of gentlefolk could thus adorn his parlance with such cunning turns of imagery?"

Then did Sir Launcelot clear his throat with coughing, hold up his hand for silence, try his voice with ah-h's and oh-h's, set one fist to his hip and the other to his chest, spit, breathe deep, and in these and other ways make ready to tell his tale.

In those dim and distant times, the Paynim Gods held sway and did amuse themselves by interfering in the lives and fortunes of men to such extent that the chiefest of these Gods, King Zeus d'Olympus, did oft and again descend to earth to partake of a maiden or two. But to confound his wife, the wonderfully jealous Queen Hera, the King did exercise his magic and make himself into the form of an animal, and thus guised did he consort with Greek maidens, now in the shape of a bull, now as a swan, and upon occasion as a unicorn, for which reason doth that animal have only one horn, but that a marvellous versatile tool.

So oft did King Zeus besport himself in this wise that Greek maidens came to prefer the swiving of beasts to that of men, and in revenge the Greek men bethought themselves to act likewise, and thus they took to the calling of shepherds, wherein such practices are not uncommon.

But the jealous Queen Hera did fume and grind her teeth at the sportings of her husband, and she did study how to work mischief upon his favored people, the Greeks. To this end did she cause Sir Paris de Troy to become enamoured of the Lady Helen, she whose beauty was rare and renowned, despite her practice of launching ships with her face.

Now know you that the Lady Helen was wife to Sir Menelaus, but he was a Greek and did consort with sheep, so she was unsatisfied with him and did accept the overtures of Sir Paris, who gave her the apple from the Garden of Eden, in return for which she did run off with him to the castle of Troy.

Now Sir Menelaus was wood wroth at this and did gather around him many knights and brave. And they did journey unto Troy to amuse themselves with the sacking of the castle, the killing of its men, and the raping of its women. But some of those Greeks, their appetites diverted through the habit of the sheep, did offer to kill the women and rape the men. And there was long and angry discourse amongst them to the issue of which should be killed and which raped, until at last the wizard Socrates did bring them to honourable compromise, the gist of which was that they should kill the first ten Trojans that came to hand, whatever be the configuration of their parts, then rape the next ten, and in this way work their way through the population, so that they might not become bored. And all the Greeks did acclaim this sage and fair counsel, save for that mighty warrior Sir Achilles, who had hoped first to rape all of Troy, the men and women alike, then to have the killing of them all. And so displeased was he with the compromise of the wizard Socrates that he did sit in his tent and did pout and sulk, saying that he would have no part of the killing and raping, an he could not have it all.

Now it came to pass that some of those Paynim Gods did favour the cause of Troy, whilst others did place their wagers on the Greeks, and so balanced and equal were the magic tricks these Gods did work that the fighting ebbed and flowed for nine years, with neither the one army nor the other gaining the upper hand.

Know you that the bravest warrior of Troy was one Sir Hector, whose prowess with lance, mace, and broadsword was wonderful to see. And each morning did he sally out from the castle to work wet wonders amongst the Greeks, who, for their part, could offer him no hurt, for one of the interfering Paynim Gods had given this Sir Hector enchanted armour that was all impenetrable. And though with good will the Greeks did beat upon his helm, and with all manner of weapons, yea e'en to the battering ram, until he was deafened with the bruit of it, never could they send point or hook through his armour. And sorely wroth were they with the frustration of it.

Now, the strengthiest amongst the Greeks was Sir Achilles, who had given over his sulking and pouting in his tent, for he saw that he was being left aside and might end with having no part at all in the killing and raping. Each morning he did ride out of the Greek camp to cleave wide paths through the ranks of Trojan knights, tracing and traversing, hacking and foining, till the Trojans were full weary with the nuisance of it; yet they could work no hurt upon him, for the meddling Paynim Gods had dipped him into a magic river of sticks and stones that did make his very skin invulnerable, save that in the dipping of him, he had been held by the heel in such wise that none of the enchanted water did touch that part. And thus it was that, unbeknownst to all, he did have one place whereat he could bleed.

And whenever these two champions chanced to meet in the melee, the Paynim Gods did connive to avoid their single combat by the ruse of wrapping the one or the other in a cloud of mist that he pass unseen, save for the sly popping out of a fist or boot to surprise the other with a smart blow.

But it came to pass that the Gods did weary of this endless tournament, and did agree amongst themselves to return to their castle Olympus and leave the Greeks and Trojans to settle the thing as best they could.

And thus, when next Sir Hector and Sir Achilles did chance to encounter in the fighting, no cloud of mist confounded their battle. And wonderfully did they rain blows, the one upon the other, passing first with the lance, which brast upon the armour of the one and the skin of the other. Then did they avoid saddles and fall upon one another, first with mace, then with axe, then with sword, then with dagger, all of which weapons brake upon the steel of the one and the hide of the other, until at last they were reduced

to the throwing of stones and the shouting back and
forth of rude insults, the gist of which turned upon the
circumstances under which their mothers did beget
them and the paltriness of her pay for the plying of
her low profession.

And a blind poet amongst the Greeks did hear
these scurvy slurs and did set them down right wonderfully, that all the world might be improved by
knowing these histories.

Now know you that the Trojans did have within
their castle an enchantress clept Cassandra who
claimed rare skill in the seeing of the future. And one
night this Cassandra did steal into the chambers of Sir
Hector for some purpose or other, and in the course of
their doings, she did tell him of the dipping of Sir
Achilles into the magic stream to make his hide im-
permeable.

"But," said she, "in the deep baptising of him,
they held him by one part, and that part knew no
water and is therefore soft and willing to bleed. And
that part be his nose, whereof doth come the saying:
'to have an Achilles nose.' "

But this poor maiden was cursed in such wise that
no one did believe her foretellings, and so it was that
Sir Hector bethought himself to try the part most distant from the nose, that being the heel.

And on that same night did the Greek wizard Socrates steal into the tent of Achilles for some purpose
or other, and in the course of their doings, he did
sagely advise the knight of a way to trick the bold Sir
Hector to his very doom.

And when the morrow did come, the two knights
met in single combat, Sir Hector studying how to dip
his lance in such wise as to prick the other's heel. But

as he approached his enemy, he was astonished to see
that Sir Achilles did lower his lance and fall into the
veriest paroxysms of laughter. So richly did he laugh
that he was weak with the joy of it and could not hold
his shield to the ready. Now Sir Hector was a true and
belted knight and would not take the vantage of a foe
who, through feebleness of laughing, could not defend himself. Yet was the noble Trojan right wroth to
see himself the object of Sir Achilles's merriment.

"But hold, Sir Achilles," quoth the Trojan knight
in angry voice. "What about me dost thou find quaint,
that thou dost point at me with limp finger and pain
thy very sides with laughter and come nigh to bepiss-
ing thyself for joy?"

"Nay, Sir Hector," spake out the Greek, "think
not that I would ridicule thee, were it not that thou art
rare risible."

"What? Risible? Me, that be suited in fine and
shining armour given me by the Gods and made all
invulnerable? Nay, nay, good knight! Do not persist
in this laughter at my cost, for though I cannot within
the code of chivalry send lance or sword through thee
whilst thou be weak and feeble with laughter, yet
know ye that the vows of a knight in no wise protect
thine arse from my boot!"

"Nay, brother knight, be not so hot in wrath. Let
us take up weapons and do combat upon one another.
And I vow that I shall try in all my most to contain my
laughter." But no sooner had Sir Achilles taken up
shield and sword than did a fresh bout of laughing
come upon him in such wise that he did drop his tools
and roll upon the ground with the delicious torment
of it.

Now Sir Hector was so wroth that he did throw

himself upon the earth also, and he did pummel the ground with his fists and did kick his heels and did wail and gnash his teeth in fury and dretch. Thus somewhat satisfied, he did calm himself and stand again to his feet, saying, "Nay, do but tell me what aspect of my appearance doth amuse thee so damnably."

"Tis in truth but a small thing. Tis that impenetrable helmet given thee by the Gods that does so tickle me. A passing bird hath shat on it, and right prettily art thou decorated with this second gift from heaven!" And so saying, Sir Achilles did roar afresh with laughter.

In deep embarrassment Sir Hector doff'd his helm to repair the blemish with the sleeve of a squire. But when his head was bare, the perfidious Sir Achilles suddenly leapt forward and with his sword did cleave him to the eyes. For know you that this had been the cunning counsel of the wizard Socrates.

And Sir Hector, seeing himself wounded unto death, did piteously sink down to the earth and lie there all unmoving. And all the knights did gather round him, those of Greece no less than those of Troy, and all did grieve to see the end of so glorious a knight. And as brave Sir Hector felt his life flowing out towards Limbo, he spake in low and rare sad voice. "Ah, my friends and foes, know you that my end be at hand. But I would not die with curses on my lips. I do confess myself beaten by the craft of good Sir Achilles, for cunning, as much as might, doth ornament the warrior's art. Mine eyes do dim, and all before me does offer to fade and swim. I would hap-

"As Hector approached his enemy, he was astonished to see that Sir Achilles did lower his lance and fall into the veris' et paroxysms of laughter."

pily die, did I but know that mine erstwhile adversary bore me no ill will, nor thought to speed my way to dark Hades with jeers and curses."

And hearing these gentle words, the heart of Sir Achilles was heavy, and he did betake himself to the side of the fallen Hector and did weep mightily.

The dying Trojan spake feebly. "Are these tears that do fall upon my brow, or be I yet again the target of a passing bird?"

"Nay, good knight," quote Sir Achilles in heavy sorrow. "Tis thy former foe that stands beside thee, giving his tears as the coins for thine eyes. O, alack that I should see this day!"

"Nay, curse not the seeing of the day, for mine eyes dim so that I can nothing see. Stand close beside me, dear Sir Achilles, a guide and sentinel on the dark voyage I must take."

"I am here, standing at thy very side," said the Greek knight with a heart-deep sigh.

"Good!" And with wondrous suddenness did Sir Hector spin on the ground and set his teeth into the heel of Sir Achilles, biting deep through boot and stock and making blood to course from that knight's one vulnerable spot. "There!" cried he. "Take that, thou lickshit perfidious bastard! And let it be a lesson to thee!"

And with these words did noble Hector sink back and die, a smile upon his face.

Though Sir Achilles allowed himself to be borne to his tent to have his wound attended to, he did scoff and say twas but a paltry blessure. And indeed the barbers and leeches of the Greek army did concur in this, but fearing to do nothing lest their fee be at risk, they did anoint the scant scathe with a healing balm of river mud and adder venom.

Upon the next morn the doctors were bewildered to discover that the knight pretended to feel no whit better than before. So they did consort together and, after deciding to double their fees to the end of doubling the value of their counsel, they reasoned that they could return him to health by ridding him of the diseased part. Thus did they take up a trenching tool and whack off the foot at the knee, though the knight did make wonderful complaint thereat.

But lo, the dawn brought no great bettering of the knight's estate, and so low were his spirits that, when he was invited by his fellows to join in the sport of foot-racing, he made courteous apologies and absented himself to his tent. And there he did die . . . from lack of exercise, was the verdict of the doctors and leeches, who sighed and shook their heads, saying that not even the craftiest arts can save a man against his will.

Now know you that the death of these two mighty knights did in no wise put an end to the battle of Troy, though the sport of it was somewhat diminished. The Greeks did ever study how to enter the walls and put that mighty castle to the torch, and it was through the counsels of the wizard Socrates that they came upon a plot so low, so vile, so foul that it has served as a model for statesmanship ever since.

Know ye that in the camp of the Greeks there was a wonderous vast horse, such as would make three of your common stallions. And such appetite did this giant horse have that fully a third of the Greek army was at all times occupied with the gathering of fodder for it. Now this wizard did bethink himself of how to rid them of this burdensome rapacious horse and, at the same stroke, take the castle of Troy. He required that five of the smaller knights don their armour and bind stalks of grain about their bodies and stand unmoving in the very place where they were wont to leave the horse's fodder, all the while imitating the sound of sheaves of grain to deceive the horse. Seeing so fine a feast, the great stallion did bound to the place and did gulp down the five faggots in such greedy wise as not to harm them with the chewing of them.

Seeing this well done, the wizard Socrates did advise the Greeks to feign that they were weary with the fighting and would retire from the lists with the matter all unsettled. Thus, the Greek host did make much noise and clamour with the taking down of their camp. To deceive those who watched from the ramparts of Troy, they called to one another in high voice, saying, "Well, well. Here we are, departing, as we are weary with this fighting and would retire from the lists with the matter all unsettled. And I tell you further, fellow Greek, though I hope I am not overheard, that this is no trick or cunning ploy, and he be a caitiff lickshit who thinks it so!"

So saying, they made great fuss and ado about departing, but in truth they concealed themselves behind a hillock to watch, leaving the fine giant horse behind in such wise that it seemed to be an offering to the Trojans who had withstood them so long and bravely.

And when the Trojans saw the Greeks retire, they did rejoice, for they knew from their own subtle overhearing that this was neither ploy nor cunning trick, and that anyone who thought it so confessed himself to be a caitiff lickshit. And several of them sallied out from the gates to take the prize and bring it to the stables within the walls. And they knew it to be a wondrous beast of battle, for when it walked it did clatter and clank as though its very bowels were made of armour.

Then did Cassandra, she who was blest by the Gods to foresee the future, but curst never to be believed, run forth from the castle and plead, saying, "Nay, fellow Trojans! Leave this beast where it is, for I do have a vision that this be a scurvy trick of the Greeks who would have this giant stallion to the stables to mount our common mares and do them brutal, if joyous, damage!"

But, true to her curse, they heeded her not and brought the horse within the very walls of the castle, where all were making grand preparations to feast and frolick in honour of their victory.

Night fell over scenes of gorging and wine-swilling. And when they kenned that time enough had passed, the five knights within the great horse did kick and strike about in such way as to give the horse rare discomfort, to the relief whereof, the beast gladly shat them out. And when these knights were espied rising from the steaming mountain of dung, the alarum was raised within the castle and all the Trojan knights doff'd strumpet and don'd armour to do battle. But when they saw the five Greek knights advance, filth clinging to all parts of them, the Trojans fell back, fearing to grapple in close combat. In their disgust, they did cast open the doors of the castle that some portion of the stench might escape. And thus was the host of Greeks lurking without allowed to pour in and do dire damage, setting torch to the city, sword to half the people, and pissette to the rest.

Great and glorious was the hacking and slaying, and in no wise less vigourous was the raping, of which many tales were later told, some beyond the limens of verity. But there be two tales of the raping that are universally attested rood-true.

While all the people of Troy did scamper and hide to avoid the raping, save for some few hags who did protest long and loud in hopes that they be noticed, the enchantress Cassandra did walk calmly through the city. And when she was stopped by a body of Greeks who did offer to rape her if she would but await her turn, she told them she had no fear in that regard, for she had had a vision that she would escape this dishonour. But, as her curse would have it, the Greeks did not believe her, and they did rape her right thoroughly.

And on the fourth day of the raping it did come to pass that the wizard Socrates was discovered in the guise of a Trojan, standing in a queue of those awaiting to be raped. And the angry Greeks did remember his foul trickery by which they had won the castle and felled noble Hector, which ploy, though it had been useful, they accounted beneath the contempt of a chivalrous knight. So it was that they condemned the wizard to die through the drinking of hemlock. And know you that in the spot where he breathed his last a tree did spring up, and they named it hemlock in honour of the poison.

In this way, through trickery and connivance, did great Troy fall, and such Gods as had erstwhile favoured the cause of the Trojans were wroth at the losing of their heavy wagers. Their ire fell upon that Paris who did give rise to all this holocaust through lusting after fair Helen, and he was transported in punishment to a distant wilderness and transformed into the city that bears his name, where dogs were made to shit in his streets in such profusion and free-dom that no traveller, even to this day, may walk with-out his eyes be always scanning before him.

Another Trojan knight saved by the Gods was Sir Aeneas, whose adventures have been sung by that right fine bard Virgil, and would be but slightly im-proved by the retelling of them here.

Long did Sir Aeneas wander in search of a fair land in which to settle, and, finding none, he went to Italy instead. But his son, Sir Ascanius, did continue the quest, and so did his grandson, Sir Silvius, and the great-grandson, Sir Brutus. It was this Sir Brutus who did at last find the perfect Albion, where he did rule in the city he founded and named Trojanova, which is in the vulgar tongue New Troy, which through usage came to be called Trinovantus and, at last, through rare marvellous error of spelling, London.

And the descendants of Brutus did reign in peace and prosperity for many centuries, now and again practising their skills at arms against the barbaric pawky peoples of the north, who, though they seldom won a battle, yet bethought themselves wonderous fighters; and who, though they were forever quarrel-ling and bickering amongst themselves over trifles, did ever seek to have the ruling of themselves, though they be not suited for it by nature nor by gift.

In the levelling ebb and flow of fate, this age of

gold passed into Time, to be followed by an era as
dark as the other had been brilliant, and the land fell
into chaos. For it was in the narrow natures of the
artisans and lower peoples of this land to despise
doing fair work for fair gain, and they were willing to
toil only to the goal of becoming masters, in such wise
that they would work only to rule, when they did
work at all. And so did they fall into the vice of scorn-
ing labour that they would have gone without food
and shelter, had they not the bounteous dole of their
masters. But in the etching and eating of time, the
properties and holdings of these masters were con-
sumed and wasted by this dole, so that they could not
maintain even themselves, and they fled to live in
France and Spain, that they might avoid heavy taxa-
tion. And in this wise all who had such gifts of mind
and spirit to direct the land fled it instead; and bitter
times fell on Albion; and the slight work the artisans
deigned to undertake was so badly done and tardily
that peoples in other kingdoms did scorn to have British artifacts about them, and commerce did fade, and
all the land went dark and cold.

And in this sad estate did the land languish until
came to throne the great King Arthur and his right
exemplary Knights of the Table Round, of whose
deeds and virtue I shall sing, directly I have eased my
voice and invention with the drinking of wine.

"A right fine tale, I do avow!" proclaimed the
Baron. "And much beguiled was I with the hearing of
it! Yea, Sir Launcelot, thou knowest well how to take
a tale by the throat and squeeze the very life from it.

Tis a gift I full admire. Most did I giggle at the merry moment when the knights were shat from the horse. But hold! Whither offerest thou to go, good daughter? And you, priest? Surely you would not abandon the table when the tales do flow so freely and well!"

The young priest explained that the maiden had whispered to him, saying that she would again and further be confessed.

"But surely, daughter," complained the mistress, "since last thou wert shriven, scarce hast thou had time or opportunity to gather up a soulful of sin."

"True, dear mother," said the daughter as she took the priest by the arm, "but so blissful was it when the spirit of God entered into me that I would fain know that joy again, as if feasting did but heighten hunger, for such is the nature of God's grace that one may partake of it oft and again, yet be not cloyed."

"But know you, daughter," protested the mother, fixing the girl with a sharp and meaningful eye, "that I myself desired to employ this lax time between the tales with the confessing of *my* sins to the priest, seeing the happiness it did bring to you, and my soul yearning to partake thereof also." And the mistress grasped firm to the priest's other arm.

Sweetly spake the daughter as she tugged the priest to her, "Do but bide thee, good mother, and belike this young clerke's skills at confession, honed with practice upon me, will the greater be when you come to him anon."

The mother's fingers tightened white-knuckled upon the priest's arm as she said, "Yea, though thou wouldst con me so, daughter, I do fear that this man of God may so fatigue his craft upon the shriving of thee that he may lack the force to confess me in like wise!"

"Yea, but good mother—"

"Shut thy mouth, fleak!" And so saying, the mother snatched the priest out of her daughter's grasp with such force as to click his teeth, and she drew him off to the shriving place in the apartments above. Whereupon the daughter did plump down upon her chair angrily, and frown, and pout, and suck her thumb, and in these ways and other ways display a want of philosophic calm.

And when the Baron sought to soothe her with sweet reason, the daughter offered him a gesture that, in a less saintly girl, might have been considered rude.

> *The Baron was amazed to see this pious rivalry*
> *Twixt wife and daughter, both of whom would fully*
> *   shriven be.*
> *He felt himself, by holiness, to be both blest and*
> *   curst.*
> *But Launcelot, who by this time had satisfied his*
> *   thirst,*
> *Did set aside his tub of wine and say that he was*
> *   prone*
> *To undertake the telling of the tale of Sword and*
> *   Stone.*

S T A V E   III

IN WHICH THE PUISSANT LORDS OF ALL ENGLAND
GATHER TO DISCOVER WHICH AMONGST THEM DOES
MERIT TO BE KING OVER ALL; AND THE WIZARD
MERLIN DOES PARTAKE IN THE CONTROVERSY
AND BRING IT TO A FAIR DECISION THROUGH
THE DEVICE OF THE SWORD AND THE STONE;
INTO THE SETTING OF WHICH TALE IS
PLACED THAT SMALL BUT PERFECT
LITERARY JEWEL: THE FEAT
OF SIR BOHORT.

ow know ye that upon the land lay
    chaos and travail
To the repair whereof did goodly
    Bishop Brice prevail
Upon the puissant noblemen to meet
in council free
That they might choose amongst themselves the man
who best would be
Equipped with wisdom, heart, and might so fulsome
as to bring
Unto that strife-torn feckless land a once and future
king.

And the advice of the good Bishop was greeted with approval on all sides, with such good will that each lord and baron selflessly offered himself to be king over all.

"Yea, though it do but increase my travail and care," said one, "it meseemeth my duty to become king over all of you."

"Nay, nay," quoth another. "It is too generous of you to offer to weigh down your life with this heavy crown. I shall myself accept the fardel of supremacy."

"Hold!" cried a third. "Think ye that I be lax in taking up sore tasks for the good of all? I will myself undertake the despised rank of king. And indeed, it would be best so, for there is some slight merit in having a king that is high-minded and honourable, and not a grasping ambitious whoreson, as are some I might name!"

"Nay, nay, fellow knight and lickshit conniver," replied a fourth. "Think ye not to plot and work that thou might come before me in rank, though I grant thou art, in some ways, the rankest of us all!"

And in such ways did they debate and probe the question at hand. But no compromise was found, though some were bruised and bashed, and here and there an eye was circled round in royal purple, as though in forecast of elevation. In the end Bishop Brice did avoid further damage by asking the lords to quit their discussions and betake themselves to the feasting boards.

Now it was during the feasting and drinking that stout Sir Bohort, he of such girth that all measurements of him were the same, did propose that a settlement of the kingship should be done by manly contest, which saying, he finished off the boar he was eating and called for another.

"Nay, nay," laughed one knight, clapping Sir Bohort upon the back. "Though I stand not against giving God the settlement of the thing through contest of arms, yet I would not have it concluded through displays of gorging, for in this high art thou art the acknowledged master of us all."

And Sir Bohort did chortle and admit twas true, for that strengthy knight could swallow as much as five men could carry, and such was his brute strength that he was wont to do battle by method of grasping up his enemy and shaking him in his armour till the poor fellow had a bruise the size of his skin. And oft did Sir Bohort foil a fleeing foe by throwing his charger at him, doing much damage to the foe, and oft some passing discomfort to the horse as well.

The merry Sir Bohort did laugh and agree that the contest should not be in skills that he alone did master. Then he did drain off a tun of wine and, rubbing his great stomach, did belch in such wise that the tent beneath which they feasted did collapse.

When it had been set again, a right lusty young knight suggested that they settle the matter with a contest of the swiving of peasant girls. And with such good will was this offer accepted that several did grasp up serving wenches and begin to practise for the tournament.

But the goodly Bishop Brice did raise three fingers in a gesture of calm holiness and quiet the tumult. And smiling gently upon the gathering, he did speak wisely to gainsay this manner of testing, saying that the accounting would be too subtle, for victory could either be reckoned by stroke or by depth of thrust, or by some cunning admixture of the two, and he did dread that long and angry quarrels might follow the award of the victory. And, although the serving wenches did complain and grumble, the generality of the knights did concur and praise the Bishop's wisdom.

Then it was that the sly and grasping Sir Dungsmere drew aside from his fellows and began to plot how to have the crown for himself, by foul means if possible, by fair if need be. For know ye that this Sir Dungsmere was as crooked in mind as he was in body, and was straight and strong in only one thing, that being his ambition.

Now, know ye that while these puissant lords were holding parley in this wise, there rested beside the road not a league away the cart of an aged wizard, one who gained his bread by the selling of potions to townsfolk, and through vending the services of a right vigourous and frick wench of eighteen summers who travelled with him. And along the road some months before they had found a stripling lad of fifteen years whom they did take with them to do low work. And the wizard's name was Merlin; and the wench's name was Gwen; and the stripling's name was Arthur.

And know you also that this old wizard carried in his cart a cunningly wrought machine that he did show to his gain at fairs and fetes. This sly engine was in the shape of a rock, but all hollow, that the wizard might cache himself within. And through an orifice at the top of the rock passed a rod of iron in such wise that it could enter and be withdrawn easily enough, unless the hidden wizard set it into clamps which prevented its being withdrawn by any force of effort. It was the practice of the wizard to gain coin at market-places through the employment of this rare cunning engine, whilst he awaited the wench Gwen's accomplishing of such exercises as he had that day arranged for her. And truly she was often long and slow in the doing of her chores, for she was a full-blooded and healthy lass who did take joy in her daily burdens, and often she gave double service for her pay, and many times did she offer samples to such men as tarried, uncertain to purchase or not. And by this practice she did cost Merlin some profit, for it sometimes came to pass that, after sampling thrice or four times, the villager would decide himself not in need of her service, and thus were time and effort lost.

Now, it was the task of the stripling lad Arthur to connive with Merlin in the working of his sly engine in following wise. Idly would the boy set and withdraw the rod of iron from the stone, wherewithin Merlin had cached himself. Then would the lad challenge some passing stout peasant, saying, "But see the strength that I have in the setting in and taking out of this rod from the stone!" And he would do so, using only two fingers.

And the peasant would scoff and answer, "Nay, thou must be feeble indeed to brag upon so slight a skill."

"Call it slight, an thou wilt," would Arthur say, as though he were little interested in this passage of talk. "And perhaps that plump damsel on your arm does bethink you manly because of your scoffing talk. But," he would say casually as the peasant made to walk away, "tis more than *thou* canst do."

And the brawny peasant would laugh and call to all about to witness how this stripling lad did boast over so fragile a skill.

"Nay," would Arthur say, "an thou wouldst scorn me, then know that I dare to wager a farthing that thou canst not withdraw the rod. If thou hast coin to match thy mouth, then set it to the wager. Or if thou durst not, then pass on thy lickshit way."

And whilst the peasant dreamt of the farthing he would so easily win, Arthur would knock upon the rock, that being the signal for the old wizard within to set the clamps to the rod that it could not be withdrawn.

And with laughing swagger, the peasant would approach the rock, and with smiggers and winks to his cronies he would set his hand to the rod for to slip it out. Then would he grunt and be amazed. Then would he set his teeth and heave. Then would he strain and curse. Then would he labour and sweat. But in the end he would fall down in a faint, and Arthur would collect his farthing. And whilst the crowd ministered to the fallen peasant, Arthur would approach the stone and whisper, "Tis I, Merlin." With which, the wizard would undo the clamps, and with whistling and tossing his farthing into the air and catching it, Arthur would lightly draw out the rod and set it back, doing this again and again until he attracted the attention of the next stout peasant with a plump lass upon his arm.

In such wise it was that Merlin and his two apprentices did gain the scant sustenance that kept their souls within their bodies. But they had fallen upon hard times, for, between the chaos in the kingless land

and Gwen's right Christian tendency to give what she
might have sold, there were days when the three way-
farers fasted closely, though their religious impulses
were but slight. And it was upon such a day of fasting
that they did pull their cart a little aside into a greensward through which a merry stream did course, their
purpose to rest the horse a little and to ponder a way
to mend their tattered fortunes. Now, know you that
the wizard Merlin was not really in his last extreme,
for he kept ever by him a small bag of coins as armour
against disaster. But rather would he go to the veriest
verge of starvation than spend this last little sum, save
it be for the gaining of more, as a thirsty man might
empty his gourd into the pump to prime it for an abun-
dance of water. And it is because of this practice of
the old wizard that we have today the name "Merlin's
Purse" for those goods or strengths one holds back to
the very last; as in the case of a woman who empties
her larder to feast a wealthy relative who lacks issue,
we say that she has used the Merlin's Purse of her
food; or of the captain who directs his last reserves to
an enemy's weak point, we say he has sent them forth,
though they be his Merlin's Purse.*

As the three sat lamenting the tight and hungry
times that did make peasants clutch their coins to the
very misshaping of them, there did emerge from the
forest at one end of the greensward a fair knight full
caparisoned in armour all blazoned in scarlet, and he
did sit a stout roan. At the same instant, by rarest
chance, there did appear at the other end of the sward

* I must confess to you, good Reader, that none of the scholars
of my family have ever discovered a single use of this idiom out-
side these tales. —N.S.

another knight cap-a-pie in armour all enamelled in black, and he bestrode a stalwart ebony steed.

And the Black Knight did call out, addressing the Scarlet Knight, "God be w'ye, Christian knight and brother! I do this day sally forth in search of contest and honour, and I bethink me right fortunate to find an adversary of rank and degree worthy to test myself upon."

And the Scarlet Knight did answer, saying, "Tis happy chance that doth set us both to this greensward through which yon merry stream doth course, for I too was riding out for the sake of my fair mistress, that I might do battle in her name and thus attest myself worthy of her favour."

The Black Knight called back, "Then tis well for both of us to meet and break a lance or two in the testing of our arts and virtues." And he did make ready for the charge.

"But hold!" cried out the Scarlet Knight. "We cannot, as Christian knights and servants to the Prince of Peace, do heavy battle the one upon the other, unless there be some cause or insult that bring us together honourably."

"Yea, thou hast the right of it, Red. But I do confess me loth to curse and insult so apt and courteous a warrior as I find thee to be."

"Mayhaps I, then, should undertake the cursing and insulting of thee, though in my heart I would be sad for it."

"Nay, nay, brother knight. For if thou didst curse and insult me with invention, that would make me wroth, and belike I would forget myself in my anger

and do foul and low tricks to you, as though thou wert
a Saracen."

"What then can we do?" asked the Scarlet Knight.
"For the two of us would be loth to lose this chance
for glory and fame."

The Black Knight pondered, and he did scratch
his helm with the fingers of his steel gauntlets, setting
up such a screeching as to put old Merlin's teeth on
edge and make him curse them both under his breath.

"I have it!" cried the Black Knight. "Sayest thou
that thou art afield in the name of thy mistress?"

"Yea, e'en so."

"How then if I curse and insult *her* in such wise
that we are free to clash and do battle?"

"The very thing! Ah, now do I wot that I have a
cunning knight to face, as well as a strengthy one. Lay
on, then, with thy cursings."

"Nay, attend. Let me find sufficient insult.
Hm-m-m. How be this? Thy mistress hath so dim a
mind that she does think the rain to be the pissing of
the Gods upon mankind, and she doth, in like wise,
ever hold her nose when there be a gentle breeze.
How's that?"

"Hm-m-m. Tis true, fellow knight, that my fair
mistress hath escaped the traps and snares of learning,
but that be no slur upon her, for was not Knowledge
the fruit of the accursed tree, and was not Sir Adam
cast down for the munching of it?"

"Yea, thou hast the right of it, brother. I did but
make paltry insult. Hold a moment and let me study
how to offer thy mistress an insult more becoming to
her rank." And the Black Knight did ponder and work

his brain. "Ah!" cried he. "This will serve! Listen, Scarlet Knight, and know that thy mistress is as ugly as a toad after the hoof of my steed has squashed it upon the roadway. There now! How's that?"

"Hm-m-m," pondered the Scarlet Knight. "Thou dost wrong to limn this slight flaw in her, good brother. For, though her beauty be but meager, yet she has a lively way of conversation. And her fingers are, for the most part, not misshappen."

"Not misshapen, eh? Hm-m-m." And the Black Knight searched deep in the filthiest parts of his mind to find sufficient cause to bring them to battle. Low did his imagination plunge, and ugly. Then did a slow smile grow upon his lips with the birth of an insult so foul that he must say it quick to have it out of his mouth. He sat straight upon his black war horse and proclaimed, "Thy mistress is . . . *French!*"

With a scream of agony, the Scarlet Knight set his lance to the rest and raked the flanks of his roan with his spurs.

And the Black Knight also put his lance to the fewter and urged his charger forward. And they did come at one another with a great thundering of hooves and clattering of armour. And awful was the bruit when each lance, well set, brast upon the shield of the other in such wise that, although the sturdy knights did keep their seats by strong clamping of their legs around their horses, the stallions did buckle to their knees and roll their eyes mournfully. In a winking, each knight leapt from the saddle and ungirthed his sword, and they did stand at each other with hack and parry and did do brave and manful work in the giving and taking of blows, and such was the ringing of their

swords upon helm and armour that peasants in distant
fields lay down their tools and filed towards their cot-
tages, thinking the angelus had rung.

For a time it seemed the Scarlet Knight had the
vantage, for he did drive his noble foe back step by
reluctant step to the very verge of the wood; but then
did the heart of the Black Knight grow strong, and he
did stand his ground, and then with mighty effort he
began to hack and foin with such good will that he did
drive his opponent back step by grudging step till the
Scarlet Knight had the forest at his back.

Now all this brave giving and taking of blows did
greatly amuse the wizard's two young prentices; and
Arthur watched with fixed eye, thinking how he did
envy to try the weapons; and Gwen did watch with
fixed eye, thinking how she did envy to try the
knights. But Merlin was troubled and vexed at this
battling, for he was deep in thought to find escape
from their poverty, and the clanging and bashing of
the contest did interrupt his deep musings.

"Try that!" shouted the Black Knight, and he did
offer his foe a cunning blow on the helm that made
him reel.

"How likest thou this!" cried the Scarlet Knight,
returning a masterful stroke that did make his opponent spin.

"The devil's piss drown you both," muttered
Merlin. But he then bethought himself to speak to the
knights to the end of discovering a way to mend his
dire circumstance. Thus did he step down from his
cart and into the greensward to have parley with the
knights.

When he arrived at the ground of combat, the

Black Knight had toppled his adversary with the sly tripping of him, and the Scarlet Knight did lie on his back, receiving a rare wonderful rain of blows from the mace. Merlin knelt beside the fallen knight and shouted into his earhole, that he might be heard above the din, "Prithee, roseate hero, couldst direct me to some place of market or fair where I might offer modest entertainments?" And all the time he spoke, Merlin did wince and shrug, fearful lest the mighty blows of the mace miss their target and fall upon him.

"Nay, old man," shouted the Scarlet Knight through his beaver, "I know not such a place as you seek. Ah! That was a well-placed one! Near did my ribs break with the strength of it! Now truly, aged one, I would not be discourteous, but I cannot longer tarry in this gentle converse, for look you how my noble foe takes the vantage of my distraction to offer great hurt to my foot by setting his horse to the tramping of it."

Then did Merlin politely stand aside and watch, offering words of encouragement to both, until in the course of the battling, the Scarlet Knight had struggled to his feet and, by the subtle throwing of sand through the visor of his adversary, blinded him sufficiently that he might fell him to his face. Then merrily and with right good will did the Scarlet Knight heap blows of war axe upon his adversary, till the melody of it quite deafened Merlin, who crawled to the fallen Black Knight and shouted into his earhole, "Good even, ebony hero. I would fain not hamper thee in this vigourous passage of arms, but couldst perchance tell me of a place where tournament or holy day do be afoot, that I might display my modest talents to some profit?" And as he addressed the knight, Merlin did

*"PRAY YOU, ROSEATE HERO, COULDST DIRECT ME TO SOME PLACE OF MARKET
OR FAIR WHERE I MIGHT OFFER MODEST ENTERTAINMENTS?"*

squirm and shun to avoid the singing edge of the war axe.

"I know of none such, old man," shouted the Black Knight through his visor, "unless a small gathering of puissant peers who are seeking to find and anoint a king would serve thy purpose. O! A finely aimed blow that! Near to cracking was my spine with the force of it! Now pray you leave me, old man. For though I would not be uncivil and rude, I cannot longer occupy myself with the pleasure of this conversation, for see you how my good foe takes the vantage of my engagement to work at the crushing of my leg with that great stone?"

Then did Merlin withdraw, but not before he had roundly thanked the Black Knight for his direction. And when he returned to where his prentices watched by the cart, he did lift his shoulders and sigh, "It would seem that there is no useful occasion in this country, save for some paltry gathering of peers down the road. But let us take our way thither. We may, at least, find some small occupation for good Gwen here. Gwen! Leave that horse alone!"

They did mount again their cart and draw away from the greensward, through which a merry stream did course. And as they rode away, ever and slowly behind them did fade the sounds of grunting and shouting, of axe upon helm and mace upon shield, for as the sun did set all streaming in golden pennants behind the westward hills, the Black Knight and the Scarlet did press on with tracing and traversing, grasping and grappling, hacking and hewing, panting and puffing in the deepening gloom to prove their valour, each upon the other.

Full night it was and dark when Merlin and his companions descended down a narrow path to the camp of the peers and barons, where torches did flicker and flageolets play—

"I am shocked," the old Baron broke in, "that those assembled noblemen allowed the flageolets to play amongst them. Out upon all flageolets, I say! There is something perverse and French about such as whip themselves for their amusement!"

The beggar-minstrel stared at his host for a long moment. He closed his eyes and shook his head sadly. Then he continued his tale.

Once in the camp of the peers, Merlin and his charges found that such persons as were not disporting themselves with serving wenches were in deep discussion on the matter of who amongst them should be king, and how chosen. Some were for this way, some for that; some were for this man, some that; and some were for having no king at all, as the maintenance of him would be greater than the worth. And from group to group the scheming Sir Dungsmere dropped here a hint, there a threat, and yon a promise, all to the goal of having the crown unto himself.

Now Merlin did wander amongst the men, proffering the services of good Gwen, and studying to learn the gist and thrust of this great gathering. And when he had done so, he drew himself apart and pondered deep and long how he could turn this moment to his profit. Then of a sudden he did clap his hands

and leap up and dance about, clicking his heels together in such wise as to do himself some temporary
hurt. He limped over to where his apprentices were
waiting and spake to them, saying, "I believe I have
found a way to sail upon the tide of chance. See that
thou standest by, Arthur, for I shall have some small
instruction for thee anon. And as for you, Gwen . . .
Gwen! Leave that stallion alone! Nasty person! Now,
go ye off and find some useful employment for thyself." Then did the wizard draw from beneath his jerkin the purse he kept as a kind of Merlin's Purse, and
he did make his way to the tent of the good Bishop
Brice, whilst Arthur stood and admired the arms and
armour of the lords, and Gwen set herself to conversation with a knight, a squire, a cook, a man-at-arms, a
stableboy, a bard, a reeve, and two fellows of uncertain occupation.

Long and deep and sly was the parley between
Merlin and Bishop Brice, and late into the night did
their shadows play back and forth upon the fabric of
the tent. In the end there was a toast drunk, and disks
bearing the heads of kings did pass from the hand of
one to that of the other.

When this meeting was at its end, Merlin sought
out Arthur and together they held long and hushed
converse, while all the camp was asleep and quiet,
save for some rustlings in the bushes where Gwen
had led her troupe of admirers.

When dawn came and the first fires sent thin
threads of blue smoke up through the cool, still air,
the lords and knights did commence to stagger from
their tents, scrubbing the sleep from their eyes with
their fists.

One amongst them suddenly cried out! The others assembled about him, and all were amazed to see, in the midst of the camp, a stone with a rod of iron through it, and beside was a plank upon which was painted in still-wet words:

I am hight Escalibore,
Unto a King fair Tresore

And when these markings had been translated by a scribe, one of the lords did ask, "Yea, well and good, but what *be* an escalibore?"

Then spake out a monk of letters and learning named Bede. "My lords, were you but trained in observation and deduction, as I be, you would know that an escalibore is either a stone, or a rod of iron, or yet a stone with a rod stuck through it." Then he frowned and wondered. "Unless, of course, it be a plank painted with still-wet words. Hm-m-m."

"Aye," said a knight. "But, tell me, saying thou hadst a fine escalibore such as this in thy manor hall, what wouldst thou do with it?"

"Twould make a rare good chair on which to seat my wife's relatives!" cried one of the lighter-hearted nobles. "The rod offering just insult to their fuds!" And all did laugh as they wandered off and set themselves to the breaking of their fasts.

After the meal, the good and wise Bishop Brice did assemble the lords together and tell them that there was a phenomenon in their midst. And full a score of them did think of the girl who had wandered into camp the night before.

"For have you not noted the miracle amongst us?" asked the Bishop, tipping his head again and again towards the stone with the rod stuck through it, and winking.

"Nay, my lord Bishop," said the monk Bede, he of letters and lore. "Pray let me make so bold as to advise you in this, as I have the good fortune to be venerable. Though the thing have the veriest look and appearance of a miracle, I recognize it to be only a common escalibore of the sort upon which one doth seat his wife's relatives."

The good Bishop frowned at the monk and continued. "Know you that in a vision I did see that there would come a great stone amongst us, and through the heart of the stone would be plunged an enchanted sword, the name of which would be Escalibore. And I did see that whosoever might pluck the sword from the stone, that person would be king above us all!"

"Nay, nay," cried out the monk Bede. "Were you but closer to this phenomenon as I be, good Bishop, you could see that this that you think to be a sword is nothing more than a rod of iron. I swear it on my venerability."

The Bishop's benevolent smile froze upon his lips and he did fix the interfering monk with icy eyes which did chill the very heart of the clerick. With a flick of his thumb, the Bishop dismissed the monk, who slunk away and returned to his task of scribbling dreary chronicals.

Then did the Bishop address the throng. "Have I not told you that this be an enchanted sword? And wot you not that a portion of its enchantment is that it can assume the shape of a common rod of iron?"

All the peers gasped and wondered, and they looked more closely at the stone. And the wily Sir Dungsmere, as he made as though to examine it, gave a secret tug or two upon the rod.

"Now," quoth the Bishop, "shall we try and learn who amongst us may prove himself the anointed king?"

The grasping Sir Dungsmere leapt forward and demanded to be first to essay the plucking of the sword from the heart of stone. And this was laughingly granted by the other lords, for know you that Sir Dungsmere was but a puny knight, and it was said of him that his bones and skin did have so great an affection for one another that they would not let flesh come between them. So this knight wrapped his long thin fingers about the rod and did tug and pull at it for some time and in many postures, but to no avail, for the wizard Merlin was cached within the stone and had well set the clamps so that no force could move the rod. At last, in his fury, Sir Dungsmere cried out, "Bah! Tis child's play! No knight worthy of his spurs would waste his force on it!" And he did fetch the stone a kick that harmed his toe in such wise that he did hop about right quaintly as the other knights clapped rhythm to his dance, and he did curse more manfully than he had pulled.

The assembled peers, by turns, sought to match their brawn against the rod, and though some worked lustily and others cunningly, they in no wise nor by an inch caused the stone to release its grip on the rod.

Now, while all this was happening, the young Arthur walked about on the edge of the gathering, and he did roll his eyes and smigger at the efforts of the knights, and did with shrugging of his shoulders and pursing of his lips seem to say that if *he* should bother to take up the task, it would be quickly done and easily. And he fell to the practice of calling others "vassal" and "low person" in such wise that, if they had not thought him a mere foolish lad, they might have set their boots to his fud.

Now Sir Dungsmere did observe the anticks of the stripling lad, and he began to fear that there might be some slight danger in his swaggering and boasting, for who would dare to behave so badly, save that he thought he might become king? So it was that Sir Dungsmere called aside three of his henchmen and to them said, "Ecoute, hench. One of you take this dagger and cache ye behind the great canopy, and when thou hearest this lowborn lad speaking on the other side, push the blade through the fabric and into his boasting flesh!" And to the second hench, Sir Dungsmere commanded, "Take up thy bow and hide ye, and when the opportunity presents itself, send a shaft through that braggart boy's back!" And to the third hench he did say, "Take this dire drop of poison from my ring and introduce it into a cup of wine, then see that it be passed to yonder swaggering lad!"

Having so arranged, Sir Dungsmere did return to the throng gathered about the stone, and he did clasp his hands behind his back, and rock up on his toes, and look up into heaven, and whistle little airs, and in every way did strive to appear without blame and all innocent.

In time Arthur did weary of awaiting his turn at the rock, for his low rank gave him priority only in such matters as hunger and toil. So he betook himself to the great canopy to seek out orts and leavings upon which to break his fast. In the queue of lower people he found himself beside a plump and fair lass, and he bethought himself to amaze her with the knowledge that she was dining with a once and future king. He did boast and swagger a little, and he felt he had somewhat attracted her, as she did blush coyly, and lower her eyes, and pant, and press herself against him, and finger his parts. But this romance was cut short by the pushing in of a brawny peasant who had himself taken a fancy to the lass. The stout peasant elbowed Arthur aside and took his place beside the tent, and the stripling was wroth and would have cursed the peasant roundly, had not the fellow chosen that moment to roll his eyes and gasp, slumping to the ground quite dead. All amazed, Arthur did run from the tent to seek aid, but as he passed through the opening, he chanced to collide with a knight, who damned him fully and drew back his arm to fetch him an instructive blow. Then did the knight cry out and stand all stiff, and complain of a pain between his shoulders, and fall back quite dead. Now the lady who had been on the arm of the knight did slump in a swoon, and Arthur ran back to fetch her a cup of re-storing wine, but when she had drunk it and thanked him prettily, she did commence to snarl and gasp and perform undignified acts, amongst which were the clutching of her throat, the foaming at her mouth, the spitting and gagging, and other anticks which she un-dertook with such vigour and abandon that Arthur was shamed on her behalf, and he would have admon-ished her, had she not taken that opportunity to roll up her eyes and die.

Then did Arthur take himself apart from the throng and noise and begin to ponder the burdens and responsibilities of kingship, saying to himself, "Take you this new fashion of falling dead all of a sudden. I see no good in it, and indeed it might do the kingdom harm, should the practice spread. If I were king, I should outlaw this behaviour as frivolous and not conducing to the common good. Also, if I were king, I should ban other habits and usages as, in the long run, do more hurt than benefit to the kingdom, to wit: hunger, sadness, illness, greed, and such sins as leads not to pleasure. If I were king, I should make good laws aimed against perfidy, avarice, and wanton chastity. If I were king. . ."

And in this wise did young Arthur take council with himself and plan the acts and laws that would make him the greatest and kindliest king this land has ever known.

When Arthur had made an end to these fertile meditations, he returned to the gathering to find that the knights had done with their essays at the rod of iron, and the commoner and lower people had lined up and did begin to spit upon their palms and flex their shoulders. But Bishop Brice proclaimed that the stripling Arthur should be first amongst the common herd, for it was growing close to the time of feasting, and his stomach was beginning to complain.

But as Arthur approached the stone, Sir Dungsmere cried out, "Nay! Hold! Before this boastful youth sets hand to the rod, there be one of rank who has not tested himself against it. And that be Sir Bohort!"

And true it was that Sir Bohort, he of great

strength and fabled appetite, had not essayed the
pulling of the rod from the heart of stone, for know
you that the cunning Sir Dungsmere had feared his
brawn, and he had arranged to divert him from the
test by setting a great table of food before him and
praying him to be guest to the feast. But now, so great
was Sir Dungsmere's hatred against the bragging Arthur that he would rather Sir Bohort be king than this
boastful snot. He further reasoned that he might connive to counsel and direct Sir Bohort in the ruling of
the country. And, if one cannot have the crown, next
best is to have the king.

All the lords called out for Sir Bohort, who was at
one time loth to quit the feasting table, and equally
loth to fail to respond to the appeals of his friends and
brothers. So he made quick work of the brace of sheep
with which he had been quieting his hunger, and he
betook himself to the place of trial against the rod,
bringing along a spit of fowl to nibble upon.

When he did look upon the task before him, he
shrugged as though it were but a paltry thing, and he
did blush when all cried out for him to exercise his
strength, but he did smile also. For know you that Sir
Bohort was a jolly fellow and, although nothing loth
to show off his arts and puissance, he was also some
ashamed that other men were feeble beside him, and
he did sorrow for them thereupon. Finishing off several capons and a pig, he approached the stone and
lightly placed his hand upon the rod. And when it did
not yield to his first tug, he frowned and scratched his
head. Then did he pull again and with somewhat
greater effort. And yet the rod came not out. Then did
someone in the crowd laugh and call out, asking if the

task be too great for a tunbelly. But the sneerer kept well to the cover of others, who, though they snickered, kept their faces bland.

Now was Bohort shamed by his failure, and also he was somewhat wroth. So he did grasp the rod in both hands and pull at it with such good will that the stone was lifted from the ground. Then did he shake it and swing it around; and he did dash it against tree trunks and scrape it along the earth; and did bash it here and there as his invention directed.

Know ye that poor Merlin within the rock thought an earthquake had come. And when he felt himself lifted and shaken and dashed against trees, he was sorely bruised and affrighted, and he grit his teeth and clung within the stone with fingers and toes, like a cat cast upon a tapestry. Gladly would he have released the clamps and ended his torment, but he durst not, for fear that the rock would fly arcing over the trees and crash to earth far away, doing him mortal hurt. So he did cling, his eyes round with terror.

At length weary of shaking and slamming the stone, Sir Bohort placed it again upon the ground, and he did stop for a time to gather breath and to partake of a tun of wine and some small joints for his refreshment. Then did he stand eyeing the stone with a scowl. Then did he spit upon his hands and take the rod in a firm grip. Then did he set both feet to the stone. Then did he pull till the veins stood out on his neck and his great girth did tremble with the effort. And many who were there later testified that the rod became longer and thinner with the pulling.

His teeth bare, his head thrown back, his great

bulk all strained to the utmost, Sir Bohort threw the last of his might into the pull.

Then it was that Sir Bohort performed the feat upon which his fame rests, a feat in praise of which bards have sung in halls and castles through all the lands of Christendom.

THE FEATE OF SIR BOHORT

With everie cynew straining and teethe sete in a
    groule
There came a roare like thunure fromme deape in
    Bohort's bowelle.
The grasse bynethe his noble fete turned yeolow, sere,
    and rust
And leaffes did flotter fromme the trese, all wythered
    fromme the gust.
And passing byrds felle fromme the skye, and
    waddled drunke and daysed
Amongst the fete of noblemen, hwo staggered back
    and gaysed
With horrure on the greenish fogge that soon would
    them o'erwelm.
And pannick gripped the bravest menne, the
    stallworthes of the realme.
Although they flede right willingly, a fewe did slump
    and falle
Upon the yerth where they did gagge and clowtch
    their throates and calle
To have their turments ended with a kyndly coup de
    grace,

As sworling vapoure etched and rusted armeure,
    sworde and mace.
And plowmen werking in the feldes a lege and more
    away
Did stoppe and snyff the ayre and frowne, and to
    their felowes say,
"Rude Piers, hast thou no scheyeme at all, that thou
    wouldst gryn and feign
That I, not thee, besmerched myself and made this
    rueful stayne?"
Then God in all His mersye made a breaze come
    from the east
To cleer the ayre and spare the lives of mayden,
    manne, and beeste.
But Ireland did suffer sore, with stunted menne and
    lamme;
The wethyr in that blighted isle has never beene the
    samme.
Greatte though the dammage was and vaste, it might
    have been more dyre
If nymble-witted servants had not dowsed the
    cooking fyre.

Then did Bishop Brice strive to bring calm to the
confusion and persuade the knights and lords to return to the assembly place, which they did full gingerly, pushing lesser servants before them to test the
air. As for the worthy Sir Bohort, he did laugh and
blush in wonderment at his newfound prowess, and
he offered to demonstrate this skill afresh, but all

about him clamoured and babbled that so great was his power as to require no further proof.

Once order had been restored, the good and wise Bishop commanded that the trials begin again, and that young Arthur be allowed to measure himself against the rod. With courteous bows and nods to one side and the other, Arthur approached the stone and, whistling idly between his teeth, did take the rod between two fingers of one hand and whisper, "Merlin, tis I." Then he did essay to lift the rod from the stone, but it would not move! For know you that the old wizard, closest to Sir Bohort at the moment of his great feat, lay now within the stone, overcome with a swoon nigh unto death.

Failing to move the rod, Arthur laughed nervously and tried again, repeating, "Merlin, tis I." But still the rod budged not. And some of the peasants awaiting their turns did begin to whistle and jeer.

"Merlin!" muttered Arthur between his teeth. "Tis I, for the love of God! This be no time for thy pranks!" And again he set his strength to the plucking out of the rod, but to no avail.

Then did the cunning Sir Dungsmere say to those about him, "Look you how the youth does mutter prayers to devils and evil things to assist him! I tell you there is no good to come from this stripling! I shall do the nation great service by slipping my dagger into his back." And so saying, the evil knight unsheathed his weapon and crept up behind Arthur.

By now the lad had set both his feet against the rock and was pulling with all his will, for his ears did burn with the jeers of the throng, which had begun to display its displeasure by the throwing of dungballs at him. "Merlin!" he cried aloud. "Tis I! Tis I! Tis bloody I!"

And within the rock, Merlin did slowly regain his senses and hear the cries of the lad. And quickly did he release the clamps.

And Arthur did fly off backwards from the stone, the rod in his hands. And the rod gave a great crack on the head to Sir Dungsmere, who was just behind the lad, his dagger poised for the strike. And the evil knight fell back upon his dagger and died, though not without first cursing his foul luck bitterly.

Then did all the gathering cheer and proclaim Arthur to be king above them all, and they did attest to the magic of the Escalibore that had made the cunning Sir Dungsmere to fall upon his own dagger and hurt himself unto death.

In the tumult and confusion, Merlin slipped from within the stone and, after leaning against a tree and gasping for a time, did come to Arthur and tell him to proclaim Gwen to be his queen, for know you that Merlin would hold authority over all near to the throne. And Arthur did concur; but for a time Gwen was not to be found. At last the wise Merlin espied a long queue of men of various estates that wound up through the camp, along a stream, across a lea, and up a hillock; and at the end of this lengthy snake of men was a bush that did shake and vibrate right wonderfully; and the wizard knew he had found the frick and cheerful lass.

And thus came it to pass that Arthur was king and Gwenevere his queen. And following the counsel of Merlin and the good Bishop Brice, Arthur did work to bring peace to the land. As the seasons passed, he built great castles at Carlisle, Caerleon, and Camelot, and in the last of these he did establish his famed Table Round whereunto the greatest and bravest knights did gather to feast and confect tales of valour and love.

The first of the Table Round was Arthur, and after him did come Merlin and Bishop Brice. And the first knight called to sit at the Table Round was the powerful and good-natured Sir Bohort, though there was a close contract that he should ever sit nearest to the door, and rush from the chamber whenever the temptation to perform a feat came upon him. And for his use, Arthur caused a great round tower to be erected in the courtyard, and this tower had walls three rods thick and no windows. To this day that tower stands, though the roof be feeble with the many liftings off of it.

Next after Sir Bohort came myself, thy humble servant and right cunning weaver of tales, the handsome, kind, and wise Sir Launcelot. Then did come Sir Gay and Sir Gawain; Sir Galahad and Sir Tristram—

"Tell me nothing of maudlin Sir Tristram!" the Baron of Dolbadarn cried. "I do detest tales of him and his sobbing Isoulde! It's all simpering love and such muck."

Yes ... well ... after Sir Galahad and Sir Tristram came Sir Gervais and Sir Bores. And so it was that ten of the twelve places around the table were taken. But one of the two chairs remaining was enchanted and called the Parlous Seat, for brute harm would come to any who sat in it, until the appointed knight be found to break its charm by unravelling the secret of its curse.

And in what way, and by what man, the next seat of the Table Round was filled, you shall know after I have paused to drink deep of wine and have some small refreshment.

STAVE IV

 fine tale! A merry tale!" cried the Baron, pounding the table for very joy. "And I do aver I was pleased to see that lickshit Sir Dungsmere struck down by the enchanted sword, for mark ye, brother knight, that during thy telling I came to believe that this vile whoreson wanted the crown for himself! Nay, nay, do not deny it! I have been abroad in the world and have learned to read a man's intent though it be masked by the most subtle gestures. But, taken all in all, I was most amused by that part describing the Feat of Sir Bohort. Ah, there were men indeed in those days, good Sir Launcelot. Think on't! A feat so fulsome as to make the cunning Merlin fall dazed and senseless! Now that's feating for thee! And I grieve to say that we are not like to experience such a feat again, for the good old days are passed and gone. Ah,

Sir Launcelot, older knights such as we can look back upon the crawl of Time and see that each generation is not what the last had been. There has been a regular decline in the quality of men since Sir Adam d'Eden, he of the fewer ribs. For who, amongst the frail and refined young knights of these days, could match the feat of a Sir Bohort? Not one, my friend. Not one! Nay, though they store their feating for half a year! O, these weakling youths do bethink themselves well feated can they but make a maiden blush with their puny efforts, or cause some slight discomfort at the dinner table. And not one of them—nor indeed ten of them lined up along the wall and piping in madrigal— could stun the knighthood of old England as bold Sir Bohort did. No, not though they grunt till the veins stand out on their brows! Yea, e'en though they o'er-pass the just limits of feating and shame themselves, they would not dare hold a candle to Sir Bohort!" The Baron sighed deeply and a great tear hung in his eye. "They're gone, my friend. The great days are gone." And he stared into his wine cup and pondered the lessening condition of man.

But his umber mood was broken by the return of his wife and the priest from the confessing. "Ah, wife," said he, "come and share with us these fine tales, for we are touching now upon deep philosophy." Then did the Baron start and gasp. "Good God! What hath stricken thee, priest? Thy face is all drawn and vacant, and thine eyes be hollow, thy knees limp, and see how thy hand doth tremble in the lifting of the wine cup! Preserve thyself, young man. Though zeal be a virtue in priests, yet thou must not ply to thy work so unsparingly, lest thou be wasted ere thy term of service be done."

And the daughter did concur heartily in this as she eyed the glowing mother narrowly. The clerick staggered to his chair and settled himself down with tender caution, for both his bells and clapper were rare sore with exercise beyond their wont, as with craft and force the wily wife had brought him oft to performance beyond his needs.

Seeing a chance for sport, the Baron winked slyly at the beggar, then spake chidingly to his wife, saying, "I note that yon limp and panting priest took something greater in time to shrive thee than he took with our daughter." He leaned close and squinted at his wife. "And I believe I know the cause!"

"Dost?" the wife asked, her eyes round with wondering innocence.

"Indeed I do! For all that thou art a good enough woman, thou hast years a-many upon our daughter, and sin piles up with time, like dung in a barn. Thus it was that thy soul was longer in the perfect cleansing!" And the Baron laughed and winked again at the beggar. "But be not wroth at my playful chiding, wife, nor frown and show me the fig thus, for we have tales of knights and valour awaiting us. So smile and be content! Now finish thy wine, Launcelot my brother knight, and on with the word-weaving!"

The young priest lifted his sunken eyes and saw that the old beggar was looking at him with something between scorn and amusement in his glance.

"A moment, mine host," the clerick said, scowling down on the ancient wayfarer. "I know not what falsehoods this low fellow has fuddled you withal, but I would be loth to see you gulled by a stranger to the parish. All men, learned and lewd, know that shaded King Arthur be dead these six hundred years. Thus, yon greasy-lipped beggar cannot be the brave Launcelot he claims."

"*Yet such indeed he be!*" cried a voice from the darkest corner of the hall.

All were startled affright, and nape hairs did prickle up as each did gawk about in wonder at this ghostly attestation.

Then it was that the hag they had taken in, and quite forgotten, waddled forth into the light, her body bowed over her dog-cudgel and the flickering flambeaux working wonderfully over her ugliness. "Yea, verily do I affirm that yon misfortunate knight is he that once did sit in pride and beauty upon a snow-white stallion, the sun glinting off his silver armour, his plumed helm under his arm, and his fair soft locks rippling gold in the gentle breeze. He is in truth and deed the veriest Sir Launcelot du Lac!"

"Ah well," said the Baron, "that settles the matter. Now let's get on with the story-telling."

"But hold!" cried the priest. "Good host, dost thou not sense some connivance here?"

"Nay," quoth the Baron. "Maugre thy doubting penchant, lad, I find myself persuaded by the hag's description. For look ye, do but take yonder bony beggar-knight and imagine him younger and handsomer by far, then let thy fancy put many pounds of meat to his frame and a foot to his height, and do but place teeth into his head and cover the naked pate with locks that ripple gold in the gentle breeze, then clothe

him all in silver armour, and voilà! Thou hast the very
image of Sir Launcelot she described!"

"But," persisted the priest, "how can this sere
and rare ugly hag claim to know who is Sir Launcelot
and who is not?"

"As to that," said the hag, a great tear starting out
from her eye and coursing the long uneven way down
her nose to hang at its tip, a transparent wart amongst
the opaque, "as to that, ken ye not who *I* be?"

"Verily," admitted the Baron, "I took thee for a
hag, and somewhat more ugly than thy calling required."

"Ah," sighed the crone, "I blame thee not for so
mistaking me. Doubtless my long history of woe and
travail has robbed me of some portion of my beauty."

"Indeed, madam," affirmed the Baron compassionately, "thou hast been pillaged to the very bone."

"Yet dare I to hope that Sir Launcelot here will
remember me, should he look long and well into my
face."

Behind his hand, the Baron spake to his wife, saying, "The poor fellow is called upon to undertake a
task more dire and painful than any assigned to that
noble knight Sir Hercules."

The beggar-knight looked deep and narrowly into
the eyes of the hag. Then of a sudden did he clap his
hand to his brow and cry, "Nay! Say it not! Is it truly
thee?"

"Yea," admitted the hag with a sob, "'tis even I,
brought so low as thou seest me before thee!"

"Nay, but—surely it cannot be *thee!*"

"I assure thee, noble Launcelot, it is indeed I!"

"Alas," sighed the beggar, turning to the Baron.

"It is truly she! It is the veriest she! It is she and no other!" And born down by the weight of this final irony, he did drop onto his bench and put his hands over his face.

"Who in God's name *is* she?" cried the Baron.

But old Launcelot shook his head and kept his eyes downcast. "She must needs tell you herself, my fellow knight. For truly I cannot."

Then did the hag cry out and beat her breast, in which part she could do herself no great injury. Then did she sob and moan and complain against the bitter fate that had brought her so low.

> *"Yea, yea, I know. Damned shame, I'm sure," the*
> *Baron did avow.*
> *"But ere my wrath dost thou some harm, pray tell*
> *me who art thou."*
> *She held her barren head up high and evenly*
> *proclaimed,*
> *"I am she . . .*
> *that once was styled . . .*
> *the beauteous Elaine!"*

"Elaine!" cried the beggar-knight.

"Launcelot!" cried the erstwhile hag.

And they fell into each other's arms, as the Baron had feared from the first they might.

"Well, there we have it," said the Baron to the priest. "What more proof could you ask than the pledge of a noble knight and that of a fair maiden?"

The young clerke rose up in protest. "Good mine host, canst thou not see—"

But he was arrested by bony Launcelot, who spake forth. "I wot there be those still unwilling to believe the word of a knight of the Table Round. Though this mistrust aggrieve me sorely, yet will I, in the spirit of trial by fire, allow the testimony of this goodly priest to decide the matter. If he humbly seek the guidance of God and, upon consideration, pronounce me true and approved knight these many years suffering under dire enchantment, then my basin shall be kept full of red wine, and my fair damsel here shall be clothed and feasted as I have been."

"And if he denounce thee?" asked the mistress.

"Ah, if he denounce me as a base and false trickster, I shall allow myself to be beaten from the hall. Yea, let the strongest of thy servants take up the fair Elaine by her ankles and club me with her, thus punishing us both at once."

"Hm-m-m. Twould be a lively sight, at that," mused the Baron.

"But whether the judgement go for me or against me, I hold myself duty-bound to repay the kindness thou hast offered me with the telling of tales. If I be adjudged a true and noble knight, then shall I regale you with noble histories of Arthur and his knights. But if I be found a low and lying knave, then shall I tell stories appropriate to my station, tales of low lust and foul deeds involving slatternly women of all stations, yea even tales of priests who enter into homes under the guise of holiness to plunder the treasures of their womenfolk. It is for thee to decide, good priest, and as thou ponderest thy judgement, recall the words of that Roman philosopher Plautus: 'He is a great fool who plots to have the bed all unto himself by shitting in it.' " And with this the beggar-knight bowed his head and humbly awaited the judgement of God as interpreted through His agent on earth.

"Hm-m-m," pondered the priest, stroking his smooth chin and frowning in deepest thought. "Hm-m-m. A moment! Slowly do I see a dim light in my memory . . . now I do bethink me—Yea! I *do* recall pious teachings that spake of the knight Launcelot and the maiden Elaine being placed under a wonderous spell that did reduce them to the foul estate of low, diseased, caitiff blackmailers, condemned to wander the earth garnering their scurvy existence by guile and craft and swinish threats of exposure."

With this, all were satisfied, and with great show of courtesy did the Baron command that the fair Elaine be clothed and feasted. Then did they cheer one another with bumpers of wine and wish one another long life and great good fortune. And though he fretted and grumbled, the priest soon succumbed to the fatigues of his unwonted exercise and fell asleep in his chair.

"Now the irksome business of proving thee a knight be aside, good Sir Launcelot," the Baron said, "do favour us with another tale to while away this night."

Then up spake the fair Elaine, she who had until lately pretended to be an ugly hag. "If Lance would rest his voice and wit for a season, I would essay to set my modest maidenly skills to the telling of a tale that might divert thee well."

"Pray do," invited the Baron. "And will it be the tale of the enchanted Parlous Seat that doth harm to any who attempt to set fud thereunto, unless he know the trick of the enchantment?"

"Nay, good host. By use and custom, that tale comes last. I shall tell thee of the encounter between Sir Gay and Sir Lionel, who clashed in heavy combat for the sake of their maidens."

"Ah, the very thing!" proclaimed the Baron.

And so it was that Elaine, she whose beauty was wonderously disguised, set to the telling of the tale of Sir Gay, Sir Lionel, and the Maidens.

Upon a time King Arthur did assemble all the knights of the Table Round to tell them that he must be apart from them for a while, for the king had undertaken to conquer the Irish islands and force peace upon those vague and tiresome peoples. For know you that there was constant strife in that benighted country, where no man said what he meant and no man trusted his neighbour, and so sly and indirect was their speech that it had no use as a language and was thought, therefore, to be a kind of literature, and every man who was incompetent with prose was accounted a poet. But their common love of story-telling and their shared hatred for work did not, as one might imagine, bind the Irish together. Indeed, they fought constantly. For there were some amongst them who swore to lies by looking over their right shoulders towards Rome; and there were others who attested to falsehoods by looking over their left shoulders towards Canterbury. And the right-shouldered Irish were the dire enemies of the left-shouldered. And each faction strove to prevent their children from commingling with the children of the other, lest the offspring be persuaded to other-shoulderedness. Oft and again did the Right meet the Left in lengthy combat consisting largely of shouted insults and cowardly ambushes; and the prize over which they fought was Ireland itself, the loser having to take it.

So it was that Arthur thought it his Christian duty to subjugate the people and force upon them the bitter fardel of peace, though both Merlin and Bishop Brice did warn him that England might become entangled in their endless and convolute jealousies and bickerings.

Before departing with a dozen men—which number he considered adequate to the task of subduing these people—King Arthur assembled his knights to urge them ever to continue their Quest for the Holy Grail, for down that path and down no other lay fame and glory.

Now know you that not one of those knights was certain in his heart exactly what a grail was, save that it was Holy and the object of Quests; but as no man durst confess his ignorance, each bethought himself the only one so stunted in knowledge, and each did always nod profoundly and sigh whenever the Grail was mentioned, and when each looked about and saw his fellows nodding and sighing right meaningfully, he was confirmed in his belief that the thing was commonly known by all save him.

To the end of slyly discovering the nature and shape of a grail, that he recognise it should he come across it in the course of a Quest, the clever Sir Gawain did nod his head and say, "Tell me, fellow knights, have you ever considered what you would do with a grail, were there one upon this table? I speak not, of course, of a Holy Grail, but rather of the common sort of grail that we all know so well."

"A grail here on the table?" asked Sir Bohort, who had not caught the beginning of Sir Gawain's speech over the noise of his gobbling down a beef.

Then did Sir Gawain pale in the fear that a grail might be too vasty a thing to be placed upon a table. "Nay, did I say table?" he asked, laughing at his misspeech. "I meant, of course, a courtyard. I do oft and again confuse the two, for are not both of them . . . things?"

"Yea, but tell me, Sir Gawain," asked Sir Galahad, hoping himself to discover slyly the meaning of a grail, "why wouldst thou put a grail in a courtyard? And what wouldst thou do with it, once thou hadst it there?"

Now was Sir Gawain full sorry he had introduced the matter and opened himself to accusations of ignorance, if not impiety. "Why should I not put a grail in a courtyard, brother knight, so long as it be a proper courtyard for the receiving of a grail? Why art thou testy in this and challenging of my motive?"

"Nay, brother of the Table Round, wax not hot in dispute. I would merely know how thou wouldst use, or wear, or kick a grail once thou hadst it in thy courtyard."

"Use? Wear? Kick?" asked Sir Gawain, now angry, confused, and shamed. "Thinkest thou I be the kind of low fellow as would use and wear and kick my grail just because I had it in my courtyard? May not one put his grail into his courtyard with no such designs upon it? Challenge me further in this matter and I shall surely have my boot into thy fud, thou base, Saracen-loving, lickshit, dungmunching bastard!"

"Saracen-loving? Saracen-loving! Now hast thou brought thy warty nose into close jeopardy from my fist, thou scrofulous, leperous, lecherous, stenchy, trull-swiving, back-stabbing, hag-foining—!"

But the wise Bishop Brice did raise two fingers in peace and pray the knights take rein on their manly tempers, and save their force for the Quest of the Holy Grail. And Arthur asked which amongst them would pursue the Quest whilst he was away taming the Irish.

Then Sir Gay, he who passed his days in the smoothing of his golden locks before a glass and in the doffing and donning of garments borrowed from Queen Gwenevere, rose from his padded siege and answered Arthur, saying, "Fear not, sire. Whilst thou art engaged in bashing those naughty Irish, the Quest will not wither. For I myself shall don armour and ride out right pertly, seeking to bring that trophy to this hall . . . or courtyard."

And all the knights did applaud and cheer, for know you that they were full weary of seeking the damned thing in every corner of the kingdom. Only Sir Gawain failed to join in the general praise, for he sat muttering darkly, "Hag-foining? Hag-foining? How did he learn of that episode?"

"We thank you, good Sir Gay," said Arthur. "And we are full aware that the realm could not have a prettier champion to undertake the Quest. But tarry you a little before you depart, for yonder comes my queen, and she would have you carry her favour upon thine adventure. Ah, blush not, Sir Gay, at the privilege of it, for know you that Gwen has given her favour to every knight of the Table Round, save for the hearty Sir Bohort, whom she seems to fear a little."

And the queen did approach fair Sir Gay and prove her honourable affection by the fondling of his smooth and golden locks, though he be somewhat annoyed with the mussing of them thereby.

"Yea, Gwenevere," quoth the king, "thou dost well to show our love for these brave knights. Now take Sir Gay apart with thee and give him thy favour. And we would have thee— Gwen! Leave that dog alone, and do as I bid!"

And the queen took the handsome Sir Gay off to her chambers and gave him her favour, though he little wanted it and accounted the acceptance the direst part of the Quest.

Thus did it come to pass that Sir Gay rode forth from Camelot to the company of fanfare and cheers, his objective the Holy Grail.

Now he had not ridden far when he chanced upon a Knight Etrange upon a fine stallion, beside whom walked a beauteous maiden in attendance. Sir Gay snapped down the beaver of his helm and challenged this knight, saying, "Stand to thy defense, unknown knight, and prepare to give and take battle! For know ye that I am upon a Quest, and I would hone my arts and address in evolutions with thee! But thou mayest avoid the sting of my lance by telling me, if thou knowest, the hiding place of the Holy Grail."

"The *what?*" laughed the Knight Etrange.

"Nay, if thou dost dare to miff me with ridicule, then prepare to stand to combat! And he who wins shall have the horse of the other as prize!"

"Hold, brother knight. I am nothing loth to break a lance or two on thee to pass the time of day, but know ye that I cannot pledge my horse to the wager, for it is a beast borrowed from another who would doubtless bring me to the law, should I lose it."

"What nature of caitliff varlet would be so low as to drag a belted knight before the law on so paltry a pretext as that, pray?"

"Tis a relative of my wife."

"Ah," said the handsome Sir Gay, then understanding. "Very well then, what sayest thou to the setting of our armour as the prize?"

"Alas, I cannot, good brother knight. For know ye that I rose this morning somewhat hastily from the bed of a neighbour's wife, and in my rush to be upon the road, I have no other garment upon me save this suit of iron."

"Art thou claiming to be all bare-arsed beneath thy steel?"

"Arse, elbow, heel, and thigh, all bare."

"But is not the chafing a sore trial?"

"Sore indeed, brother. And it is for reason of the chafing that yonder maiden, recently won in combat, walks at my side, rather than grunts under my weight."

"I see," said Sir Gay. "And verily thou hast the right of it, knight. For I could not take thine armour and leave thee to ride the roads all 'bare-arsed on a borrowed horse,' as the old saying has it. Our shared rank and degree forfends it. Hast thou nothing of value to wager upon this encounter?"

The Knight Etrange shrugged. "Nought but this

fair and beauteous damsel, who is sure virgin but this morning won from a rogue who had stolen her from her castle, and all untouched by me for reason of the aforementioned chafing."

"And thou art offering to set thy damsel against my horse?" asked Sir Gay.

"If its withers be good and its teeth show no excess of age." And with this the knight dismounted and came to Sir Gay's horse to lift its lip, while Sir Gay dismounted and yode him to the girl to lift her skirt, which act he performed out of custom, for he little wanted the lass.

When they had mounted again, the Knight Etrange asked, "What sayst thou? I find thy horse good enough, though it be sway of back and a little blind to the left."

"I pronounce this maiden good enough, though she have but half the legs of my steed. But how knowest thou that she be a virgin? Thou hast said that thou tookest her from another knight in fair and proper combat. Belike he was amongst her bits beforehand."

"Nay, good brother. For he was in the very act of preparing to swive her when I came upon him, and he had not yet his armour off, though he was clawing at it right willingly."

"How now? Didst thou challenge him while he was in the very act of swiving?" asked Sir Gay. "Nay, nay. Is that a proper thing between knights?"

"Do not think I would treat a brother so. I did not challenge him at all, but rather crept up on him whilst he was panting and tearing at his armour to have it off."

"Ah," said Sir Gay in admiration. "A cunning and right pretty ploy! I see I have an adversary of wit. But did he not hear thee approach?"

"Not till I was almost upon him, brother. Then did he essay to run and flee, but a man loses something of his swiftness with his armour all about his ankles."

"Belike. Belike. But enough of this fair talk, knight! My horse against thy maiden! And God and Saint George be with the better . . . person!"

And they did charge down upon one another with speed and bruit, their helms forward and their lances well set into the fewters, the points directed to the fell hurt of each the other.

But never did they meet.

For at the instant their lances might have splintered each on the other's shield, both did flinch away, and they flew past each other at great and thundering speed, and good Sir Gay ran deep into a thicket of briar, which did torment the cullions of his stallion in such wise that the noble steed did snort and rear and throw off his burden, all a-clatter, into the thorns. And Sir Gay was some weary time escaping, slashing the thicket with his sword with such angry vigour that the branches might have been the limbs of unarmed and surrendered Saracens.

But twas the Knight Etrange who got the worse part of the deed, for know ye that his stallion thundered on at breakneck speed, and rushed upon a gully at the border of the lea. The knight pulled back upon the reins with such good will that he pressed his plumed helmet to the charger's bouncing rear, whilst his spur did almost hover at the panicked horse's ear.

The stallion's legs were planted stiff, hooves furrowing the ground. Yet down the steep-cliff gully did they tumble, bounce, and bound!

All mingled man and beast, they tumbled. And one did snort and the other curse; one did whinny and the other whimper. Betimes the man rode the horse, and betimes the horse rode the man. And when their merry journey was done, the Knight Etrange found himself so bruised with the riding and so fatigued with the carrying that he did lie all unmoving in a deepest swoon.

When the handsome Sir Gay had waged long and fair combat against the Ogre of the Enchanted Briar which did pluck at him and seek to ensnare him, he staggered out from the bramble and looked about to find his adversary. But lo, such were the enchantments of the place that the Knight Etrange was all vanished as though the very earth had swallowed him up. And Sir Gay did fall to his knees and give thanks to God for saving him from the spells and dark craft that had spirited away his noble opponent. And when he rose, he found his brave steed had also crashed out of the thicket, all unscathed, save that his whinnying was thin and high from the damage done by the thorns.

When the sun was high, Sir Gay with his won maiden behind him on the saddle entered upon a little greensward through which a merry stream did course, and in this greensward they did find two knights deep in dire combat, one of them caparisoned all in scarlet, the other all in black.

For a time Sir Gay sat astride his charger and watched the knights test their force and cunning upon one another. The battle went one way, and then the other, each knight delivering and receiving brave blows with sword, axe, mace, and handy boulder which rang grandly upon their armour. Then did the Black Knight seem to gain the better of the fighting, for he felled his opponent into the stream, and he sat astride the Scarlet Knight's back and laughed, whilst the other did bubble and gasp and gargle as though to suggest he little enjoyed the breathing of water.

Sir Gay dismounted and yode him to the place of combat, calling out, "What cheer, good knights?"

The Black Knight answered courteously, saying, "Good enough cheer, brother. This essay at arms does seem to go my way at the moment; and the sun be shining on this greensward; and I have the pleasure of thy company. Yea, good cheer enough."

But the Scarlet Knight answered not, save for some gurglings and bubblings, which Sir Gay could not accept as fair and formal greeting, and so he became wroth at the impolite knight, and he said, "Nay, fallen knight! Think not to pass me without greeting, nor imagine I will accept thy foolish gurglings in lieu of proper and friendly speech." And with this he fetched the Scarlet Knight a kick with his steel boot, well aimed to his dangling bits and designed to help him mend his manners. But far from being chastised and shamed, the Scarlet Knight did but flay his arms and continue with his ill-bred bubblings and gaspings.

"What brings thee to this greensward?" asked the

Black Knight of Sir Gay, as he rested from his martial fatigues astride his gurgling foe.

"In truth, dark hero, I am the prettiest knight of the Table Round, as no doubt thou canst see, and I be on the Quest of the Holy Grail."

"Nay, friend, think not to con me so. Surely no knight of wit would be such an ass as to play that ancient game."

"But I attest that the Holy Grail is my avowed Quest."

"Oh? Indeed?" And the Black Knight made so bold as to laugh.

"Nay, an thou ridiculest me, have this for thy pains!" cried Sir Gay, fetching the ebony knight a great blow with his mace to the side of the helm.

And the Black Knight toppled from the back of his foe and sat in the middle of the stream, all stunned and amazed.

Seizing his chance, the Scarlet Knight leapt to his feet and, kicking off one steel boot that the water might run from his armour, he gave the Black Knight a bash with the point of his shield that rolled him to his back, and whilst the Black Knight took up the bubbling and gurgling that erst had been the language of the other, the Scarlet Knight did greet Sir Gay, saying, "Much thanks for thine assistance, good brother. That kick to my dangling bits he offered me nigh ended my will to live and my urge to love. Is there any service I might offer thee in recompense?"

"Thou might, and thou canst, tell me where is cached the Holy Grail, for know ye that I am on the Quest thereof."

The Scarlet Knight turned his head aside and made sounds, and his shoulders shook.

"Nay!" cried Sir Gay. "Are these gigglings I hear? First gurglings, and now gigglings? Have *this* for thine improvement!" And he fetched the Scarlet Knight such a blow as he had erstwhile offered the Black, which fine bash did topple him from the back of the other. Then did both knights struggle to their feet and, when the Black Knight had doff'd his boot to the draining of his armour, they did stand together, panting and fuming, both facing the valiant Sir Gay with dark and angry miens. And they did call him names and work together to confect a lineage for Sir Gay that included only unhealthy people and lower animals. Then did they offer to unite their strengths in the punishing of this interfering stranger.

But Sir Gay yode unto them with humble voice and friendly words, saying that he had intended no interference with their trial at arms, but only sought guidance upon his Quest. And he did confess himself full regretful and shamed, had he hindered their fighting. Then with quick gesture, he trampled heavily on each of the bared feet, and as the Black and Scarlet knights hopped about, clinging to one another in a right pretty dance to which they howled rare melodious accompaniment, Sir Gay ran back to his steed and maiden and galloped away.

Now, when the sun was halfway to the westward River Ocean, Sir Gay and the maiden came upon a bridge that forded a stream. But as they made to cross, they were challenged by a knight on the other side, he also having a maiden with him. "Back away that ancient cow that serves you for a steed," shouted the strange knight, "for know ye that I would cross the stream first!"

Sir Gay snapped down the beaver of his helm and called out, "Nay, loutish knight! An thou durst precede me to the fording, I shall have thee upon the point of my lance like a spitted lark!"

And the stranger knight closed down his visor and cried, "Breathe deep, brother, and sniff the sweet air of thy last day on earth! For I am Lionel, knight-errant and the handsomest warrior in Britain! And I would this day prove myself deserving to sit at the Table Round!"

"Poor child!" scoffed Sir Gay. "That thou must die ere thou hast forsaken shitting yellow. Hear this and quake! Thy foe is Sir Gay, the most beauteous knight in Christendom, and full approved fellow of the Table Round!"

"I challenge thee, Sir Gay. And I invite thee to the middle of the bridge, there to test which shall pass first!"

"Done! And for my necessary insult to you, hear this! That scabby hag that sits behind thee is the very source and fountain of ugliness in this world, and if you got her through combat, then it must needs have been through the losing of it!"

"Nay, knight, nay! It denies thy vows of chivalry to abuse so fair and comely a princess, at all points finely made and manageable. Tis *thy* wench who is so loathsom that even my stallion does gag and grow faint at the sight of her! Thine unknightly slurs require me to mention that the diseased wineskin behind thee is surely proof of thine infinite miserliness, for it appears thou dost hoard thy shit in a bag and carry it about with thee—though I humbly beg the lady to take no offence at being thus limned, for my quarrel be not with her."

"I hold these insults to be sufficient to bring us to battle," called out Sir Gay. "Let us avoid horse and meet on the bridge!" The two knights descended from their saddles and strode over the bridge to the midmost point, their maidens following behind. And when they stood facing, Sir Gay spake out. "It were right low and unmanly of thee to abuse my delicate and high-born maiden so. For thy punishment, see now what I do to *yours!*" And with that, he fetched a slap to the blushing cheek of Sir Lionel's lady that sent her sprawling.

"O, coward! O, base person!" cried Sir Lionel. "Wouldst shame all Christian chivalry to use a gentle virgin in so scurvy a way? Then take *this!*" So crisp was the slap he delivered to Sir Gay's princess that she sat instantly to her arse and blinked in maidenly confusion, her creamy thighs all exposed.

"I cannot allow a woman to be treated thus!" roared Sir Gay. "Thou art nought but a gruff and butchy man! Let *this* be thy fell punishment!" And he pulled the nose of Sir Lionel's gentle maiden until tears stood in her eyes at the beauty of it all.

"What?" screamed Sir Lionel. "Wouldst pervert chivalry into a subtle device for the lessening of woman's station? Fie! O, base and loathsom fellow! Have *this* for thine instruction!" And he offered Sir Gay's maiden a kick to the fud of such wonderous force that she rolled head-over-heels along the bridge and

ended with her skirts about her hips and her little
shield revealed as though she would defend herself
with it.

Sir Gay jumped up and down with fury as he
cried, "Now hast thou gone too far knave! There will
be neither let nor quarter in this battle!" And he
grasped the heels of Sir Lionel's maiden and ran with
her along the bridge, her plump fine arse bumping
from log to log, till she howled with the surprise of it.

Nor was Sir Lionel idle whilst his foe worked this
mischief. He thrust the head of Sir Gay's maiden into
a fork of the bridge railing and pulled her legs till her
neck grew gracefully long.

With great vigour and invention did the knights
offer harm and insult back and forth until nearly was
it dusk and they stood panting and weary with their
exercise.

For need of air, Sir Lionel pulled off his helm and
breathed deeply. Then Sir Gay approached him and
said, "Nay, then, coward knight! Has had enough of
this . . . God save my buns! Thou art indeed the handsomest knight that ever I set eyes upon!" And he did
off his own helm in respect.

"Think not, Sir Gay, that polite words can mend
the damage that . . . Lord bless my parts! Thou art
surely the fairest knight that ever I have seen!"

And they did gaze soft-eyed on each other in admiration for some time.

Then did Sir Gay speak out, "Nay, gentle brother,
I would not offer thee further harm."

And Sir Lionel did say, "The error was mine own,
sweet friend. I should not have prevented thee from
the crossing of the bridge."

"And now I bethink me, charming knight," said Sir Gay, "twere like we both have been victims of an enchantment. For look ye, I did fight for the honour of my maiden, whom I mistook to be a fair and beauteous lass. But now I examine her more closely, I do see that she be nought but a bruised and damaged thing that I would not have about me."

"The same bewitchment has befallen me, lovely person. For she whom I took to be a jewel of rare value, I now see is but a marred and flawed thing that I would not pick up with tongs."

Then with kicks and harsh words, the knights sent the maidens running from the bridge with stern warnings never again to work their evil spells on pure and noble knights.

And the maidens, standing on the far rive, did unite in shouting back insults and showing the fig, declaring that they would never rest till womankind had risen above these useless, bragging, swaggering studs. Nor would they be content to become the mere equals of such foul, pride-wracked, shitlicking, posturing, childish, abusive, dungmunching whoresons! And they did depart arm in arm, vowing to be forever sisters in their struggle against the debasing false pride of men.

Ignoring these frail threats, the knights did turn together and, as with one will, they did clasp hands and gaze upon one other.

"Let us swear now," said Sir Gay, "never to be the one far from the other, but ever together in close and warm companionship."

"Thou hast given voice to my will," said Sir Lionel.

". . . GOD SAVE ME! THOU ART INDEED THE HANDSOMEST KNIGHT THAT EVER I SET EYES UPON!"

And they did retire a little ways into the wood, and there did they confirm their friendship in many and pretty ways.

When, some days later, they arrived back at Camelot, Sir Gay introduced Sir Lionel to the knights and did avow him to be a champion brave and puissant. And upon his protection was Sir Lionel offered a seat at the Table Round.

"But not *that* one!" cried Sir Bohort.

Too late! Sir Lionel had unwittingly sat in the Parlous Seat, and instantly did it work its harm and mischief on him, doing him stunning hurt in such wise that it was some days before his friendship with Sir Gay could continue and grow. For Lionel, brave and handsome though he be, was not the chosen knight who would one day discover the secret of the Parlous Seat and break its curse.

And thus it was that the fellows of the Table Round numbered eleven, and the twelfth was yet to arrive. And of this last knight Sir Launcelot dozing yonder will have to instruct you, for I have weakened my maiden voice and cannot continue.

And with this the fair Elaine, erstly haggish, drank deep of the red wine and rested her voice.

"An excellent tale!" pronounced the Baron. "A tale of vigour and sweep, and not overly burdened by the deep philosophy it contained. Great pity the priest has slept through it, though by his sallow face and dark eye sockets I can see he requires his rest. And now, good Sir Launcelot, give us the tale of the twelfth and last knight of the Table Round, that we

may learn of the Parlous Seat. And pray make the story
have to do with heavy battle and dire combat, along
with cunning tricks and lusty swiving. But above all
do not touch upon the tale of mewling Tristram and
sobbing Isoulde, for I do detest to hear of love and
suchlike offal."

"O, never fear, my brother knight," said noble
  Launcelot.
"Thine ear will not be cloyed with sticky gentleness,
  I wot.
For I have tales of Persival, the rudest of the knights.
No courtesy of manners was amongst this knave's
  delights.
A vulgar, low-born cur he was, the randiest of
  men."
"Ah, good. That's fine!" the Baron said. "On with
  the rudeness then!"

S T A V E V

IN WHICH, AFTER AN IRKSOME DIGRESSION INTO
MATTERS OF SCHOLARSHIP, WE LEARN OF THE
LOW ORIGINS OF RUDE SIR PERSIVAL, HIS
FAMED FLAW, AND HIS RISE TO THE
LOATHSOM RANK OF MERCHANT;
THIS BEING PART THE FIRST:
RUDE BEGINNINGS.

idely known is it that Sir Persival was called the Rude Knight. But the exact origin of this uncommon nomen is a matter of deep and acrimonious debate amongst scholars, clerkes, men of logick, bards, apologists—indeed amongst all such minds as yearn to know whither falls the falling star, or the precise number of angels one may pose on the point of a pin without undue discomfort to the bottommost. Some defend this opinion, and some that. There are those who claim that Persival was called the Rude in result of his practice of wearing armour all enamelled in red. For know you that the words "rude" and "red" do derive from a common root, in

proof of which is the fact that maidens do blush *red* when something *rude* is said at dinner.*

But not all scholars hold to this view. There are others, no less admired and praised for their skills in decorating commonplaces with ribbons of Latin, and for piecing together fragments of other men's thoughts so skilfully that the joints and cracks are almost invisible to the naked mind, who maintain that Persival was clept the Rude by virtue of his filthy habits of speech, wherein he was much given to swearing his oaths upon the nether parts of sainted persons, as in: By the damp balls of John the Baptist! Or, By the pierced balls of Saint Sebastian! And no fair-minded man can doubt the rudeness in that!

And there exists a third and equally defended school of thought that would have the Rudeness of Persival derive from his low birth. For know you that of all the Knights of the Table Round, Persival alone lacked the blood and training of a noble family. Sad to say, Persival's mother was a low wench of Lud's Towne who did vend the comfort of her thighs. And it was said of her that she passed so much of her life upon her back that she was ever dizzy and uncertain when standing upon her feet.

So there are three major streams of controversy

---

* In fact, either the beggar-knight or my ancient ancestor who gives him voice is guilty of rather shaky etymology here. "Red" and "rude" descend to us down quite separate paths, the first stemming from the Sanskrit *rudhirá* through the Latin *rufus*, while "rude" emerges into Latin as *rudis*. The two brush close in Middle Dutch as *ruud* and *rood*, but it is unlikely that Davydd ap Seare was aware of that. I fear my ancestor was engaging in that kind of nonce etymology that characterized scholarship of the Middle Ages, praiseworthy more on the grounds of imagination than research. —N.S.

over the Rudeness of Persival. There is the School of
Red Rudeness; the Faction of Swearing Rudeness;
and the Party of Common (or Lowborn) Rudeness.
And the scholars of one group do despise and scorn
those of the other, and they do ridicule and detest—

"A-a-a-argh!" roared the Baron.

Sir Launcelot, erst beggar, erster scholar, blinked
in confusion at being thus uncivilly interrupted. "I am
not sure I catch thy meaning, brother knight," he confessed.

"What care I for all this babble of schools and
parties and factions? Call the fellow rude and be done
with it, for pity's sake!"

"Ah, good brother, surely thou wouldst not have
me plunge into the tale of Persival without first acquainting you with the burning scholarly questions
that do rage around the seeming-simple story. How
else wouldst thou apprehend and appreciate the subtle meanings and symbols of the legend?"

"Let the devil piss on the burning questions and
extinguish them! And if the Fiend's bladder be up to
the task, let him wag his pissette about and piss also
upon all symbols! I give ni fig ni fart for symbols!
What I want is a good story, man! Thou hast babbled
on till mine eyes do droop, yet nothing of meat and
matter hast thou said!"

"Ah," said the beggar-knight, "thou probest to the
very heart of the bard's craft. For know ye that in the
art of word-weaving, the setting is more valued than
the jewel, the purse more admired than the coin. It is
a kind of alchemy of the imagination in which the

base matter of the tale is converted into veriest gold through the story-teller's wit, learning, cunning, invention, lore—"

"Get on with the tale, for the love of God!"

The brawling babe who was dropt Rude Percy and who rose to become Persival the Rude had, at his birth, a physical distinction that influenced his future mightily: that which some chroniclers have clept Persival's Mar, others have called Persival's Blemish, but which is most commonly referred to as Persival's Flaw.

First to remark upon this Flaw was the ancient crone who midwifed his dropping out, and she was filled with wonder as she swaddled the babe in rags. When the sweating mother, who had come to the conclusion that getting a brat out was somewhat less amusing than getting one in, asked if it was a boy or a girl she had grunted forth, the old midwife answered that it was a boy indeed, and in some ways it might be thought of as three or four boys.

"And is it healthy and well formed?" asked the mother.

"Well formed nigh to excess, deary."

"And I hope it is not flawed or uncommon."

"Uncommon it is, and more's the pity for women!" cackled the crone. "But if you call that a Flaw which dangles to its knees like the clapper of the great bell of Bow, then I do vow that I wish each of my four husbands had been similarly flawed! Yea, though I died of it, pierced to the lungs!"

It is not courteous or meet to describe the nature

of Persival's Flaw in the presence of ladies, but I will say that, although he swived and foined countless dames and damsels during his life, he could claim at the Gates of Heaven never to have touched his belly to any woman's.

Let this hint be enough, for more I cannot in modesty reveal.

Directly the babe could be tugged from the teat, his mother abandoned him as an encumbrance to her craft; and so it was that Rude Percy grew into young manhood like a weed, untrained, untended, and for the greater part unwanted. But like unto the despised weed, he flourished where finer flowers waned and wilted.

At seventeen, he was a laughing, loud, and roisterous lad who wandered the narrow and shitten lanes of Lud's Towne in search of shelter, food, and above all amusement. He conned the evil tricks of swearing and of battling with naked fists, of cadging sots and of snatching purses from swaggering gentlemen who, simpering with derision at the foulness about them, pressed pomanders to their noses and ventured into these wretched quarters to wench and riot that they might boast about it later.

Well might one ask how this beggar lad found sustenance to maintain his great growth and strength, for know you that never had he coin about him, for what he cadged or stole by day, he spent that very night, always generous and never cautious against the morrow. In truth, he never lacked for food, for there were women of Lud's Towne, and of all degrees, who had heard tales of his wonderous Flaw, and who did bring the lad in secret to their gardens and chambers to feed him with sweetmeats and viands that he might reveal to them his Flaw. And they would gape in curiosity and admiration and comment on the glory of God and His natural works. And further, once he had passed thirteen summers, these women found new ways to measure and appreciate the mysteries and miracles of God. And often, in consequence of her deep devotion to learning and measurement, was a good burgher's wife of Lud's Towne seen strolling in her garden, stiff and fragile of gait, but nonetheless humming to herself and carrying upon her face a smile of deep peace. For know ye that Science and Curiosity, though they be hard taskmasters, yet offer rewards of satisfaction.

But the merchants of Lud's Towne were not so kindly disposed towards Rude Percy. Gravely would they shake their heads as the lad sauntered past, whistling and singing, for they thought him a wastrel, a scrambler, a profaner, and a thief. They did all agree that he was but gibbet meat, bound for the hempen noose, and they did concur amongst themselves that the lad must sure be hung. And wives exchanged glances, and their faces grew red, and their eyes shone with laughs unlaughed.

When Rude Percy had sweated eighteen summers and shivered eighteen winters, he began to doubt his riotous ways, for though he was untutored, he was not without common guile, and well he knew that his loose life would more quickly bring him to grave than to glory.

"Face up to it, me fine Percy," said he to himself. "This will not do! You'll not make your fortune by bashing the heads of fops and servicing neighbour

women with your Flaw. Time has come to find yourself a snug living. It's into trade with you, by the four
and twenty balls of the Apostles!"

So Rude Percy cast about, not for an easy craft,
but for an easy craftsman. Having noted how others
rose within the guilds, he sought a master possessed
of three desirable qualities. He must be childless. He
must be old. And he must recently have taken unto
himself a young and lusty wife.

In time Percy learned of a merchant who had de-
voted his youth and middle years so fully to trade and
the piling up of coin that he forgot the softer pleasures
until an increasing softness of his own hinted that
Time was sifting away. Against the counsel of his
friends, this merchant had recently taken unto wife a
plump and frick girl for whose every year he had
three. Many were those who warned him to wear a
close cap, lest someone set horns to his head, but he
was merry and blithe in his doting appetite, and he
did hop and dance at his wedding feast with such
madcap vigour that he quite spent his force before
drawing his bedcurtains.

O, how oft is it so! And how sadly! How oft have
men whom the passing of years ought have worn towards wisdom acted as though they thought Youth a
catching disease, as certain humours are, and played
the fool under the intoxication of young flesh! Many
an eye, shrewd and narrow in the countinghouse, rolls
idiot-ogling in the bedchamber!

So giddy was the old merchant with his lass that
it was some days before he noticed a young man loitering before his door and sighing, only to run and
cache himself when the merchant looked down from

his window. The old man did fear this comely, if ragged, swain was so smitten for the love of his plump young wife that he did sniff about the door like a whelp after orts. And so it was that the merchant in high wrath accosted the youth and told him to be gone, lest he envied to feel the baillif's baton upon his shoulders.

The youth hung his head and admitted himself every low kind of wretch, and not the least a cowardly one, for although he vowed each night to summon forth courage to beg a favour of the merchant, yet each day the sight of the wife cooled his ardour and frightened him away.

"How?" asked the merchant. "Claimest thou to be cooled by the sight of my wife?"

Tears did stand in the youth's eyes. "Aye, tis so, master. For know you that women scoff and jeer at me in such wise that I have come to detest the very sight of them." And with this he laid his hand upon the merchant's sleeve with so gentle a touch that the worthy burgher stepped back and looked about, fearing the gossip of his neighbours.

"But tell me, how comes it that a lad of fair, if begrimed, countenance and strengthy, if filthy, body finds such discomfort in the company of women?"

Percy (for the loitering lad was he, and there is no point in concealing it further) let a tear fall to the paving stones before answering in low and humble voice, telling the merchant of his terrible Flaw. Upon hearing of it, the good merchant struggled with all his main to avoid a confirming glance, but he failed. And when a worried peek attested to the ragamuffin's ascertains, the merchant asked, "But how can it be that this . . . affliction . . . causes thee to shun women and flee at their approach? I should have thought thou wouldst be eager to enter the lists, armed with so stout a lance."

"And so I was, and to excess," admitted Percy. "I entered the lists night and day, and oft at noon."

The merchant quickly closed the shop door behind him, lest his wife hear of such vigour.

"Yea, master, with such abandon did I wield my Flaw that now I have quite lost the use of it and, what is worse, the desire for combat." And the strapping lad dropped a tear.

"What? Can it be that thou, by Nature so well equipped, hast lost thy savour for foining? While I . . . while I . . ." The merchant sighed and he too dropped a tear.

"Tis even so, good master. And that be not the more painful part. For know ye that the jeers and taunts of women ring ever in my ears, for many know me to be a scabbard without a sword, and they blame me for it."

"Poor fellow," condoled the merchant, though in his heart he felt a tickle.

"O, master, if only thou hadst not a young wife! Then might I dare ask the boon I crave of thee!"

"What boon be this?" the merchant asked, edging away again.

"Why, to be trained in the merchant craft at thy feet, master. To learn from thee, whom all the city avows to be wonderfully adept and skilful at squeezing each coin till the king winces."

Though he said tut-tut, the merchant blushed with pride.

"How I yearn to gain from thee the skill of buying from the starving and selling to the rich, of creating need in the midst of plenty, of sapping other men's successes and pouncing upon their failures—indeed all the merchant crafts. But I dare not ask this boon, master. For what would thy neighbours say shouldst thou take in a youth of my apparent, if useless, parts? They might accuse thee of boasting of thine own bed-craft by showing that thou needest fear no rival."

"Hm-m-m."

"And think of thy bride! Used as she is to thine attentions, might not she seek the like from me in your absence, in the charming ignorance of her virtue? And how should I explain my failing? How could I avoid her laughter and taunts?"

"Hm-m-m."

"Nay, good master, nay. I cannot ask thee to take me to prentice, bearing as I do my useless Flaw, even though I had planned to offer myself into bondage with no other pay beyond the enrichment of my craft and learning, but I wot that. . ."

. . . When he had been two months installed in the house of the merchant, Persival received the news that his master was going upon a pilgrimage to Canterbury to praise God for giving him a plump and frick wife and an impotent prentice. And this intelligence made Rude Percy skip for glee. "I've got him! I'll repay his curses and cuffs, his thin beer and thinner soup! By the perfidious balls of Judas, I've got him!"

And know you that Persival had prepared for this day. Twice had he stumbled from his bath in innocent nakedness into the path of the plump young wife, and in his confused efforts to conceal his shame, he had hidden his face with the drying rags that might better have covered his Flaw. And the wife had been left standing, stunned and round-eyed, in the hall.

On the morning of the departure, there was great noise and merriment in Southwark where the merchant and other pilgrims assembled at the sign of the Tabard across the narrow alley from the shop. All manner of men, high and low, were embarking upon this voyage to the shrine of Thomas à Becket, amongst whom was a Controller of Customs rumored to possess sixty books, new and old. And this public man, ever taking down notes upon his fellows, had a glint in his eye as he looked up at the window of the merchant's apartments and espied the plump wife leaning out to wish her husband safe journey.*

From the street below, the merchant called up to his wife, telling her not to fear for his safety and to pray for him.

Within the shop, Persival stealthily approached the wife leaning over the casement, and he lifted her skirts from behind.

"Nay, wife," called up the merchant, "weep not so, though I delight to know thou dost feel the loss of me so deeply. Know ye that I shall be in this merry company, and no ill shall come to me. Nay, nay, wife!

---

* The scholars of my family have noted a severe "lesing" in the tale here. Davydd ap Seare is describing a London of his own time, the last of the fourteenth century, and not of the age of Arthur. This fact has led us to believe that the note-taking Controller of Customs mentioned is some contemporary of Davydd ap Seare's, but sadly, the concentrated scholarship of seven generations of my family has failed to identify the man. —N.S.

Do not gasp so! Please, good wife, do not moan so! I would not have my fellow pilgrims think me hard of heart to leave so loving a girl. Console thyself with young Percy in my absence. Spend thy lonely evenings in his company, and in no one else's. And pray do not shudder so with grief and grip the casement till thy knuckles be white! Come, now! Tighten thyself! Be a brave girl, and give over all this heaving and groaning and rolling of eyes! O, look you, fellow travellers. It is a sight to turn a man's heart with pride. See how limp she is from excess of woe? See how she hangs out the window panting? Ah, there's my brave child, smiling at last! Now that is better. Satisfy thyself with the knowledge that I shall be gone but a month. O, Lord love me, there it begins again! The gasping and moaning! Come, let us be off. I cannot bear her grief longer." But as he mounted his wide and comfortable horse, he said aside to the sage Controller of Customs, "Still, it is some small pride to a man of my years to be able to affect a young wife so, do you not admit?"

The Customs Clerke nodded and smiled.

"By God!" cried the Baron, delivering the oaken table a mighty blow. "They are all the same, these lowborn moneylenders! Asses and jackanapes all! O, they're quick enough at telling the sum while any honest man is still mumbling on his fingers! And they're willing enough to lend silver to fit a man out for war! And they're mean enough to take a farm or two away from you because of some nonsense writ in small Latin! But they're fools when it comes to the

"Nay, wife," called up the merchant, *"weep not so, though I delight to know thou dost feel the loss of me so deeply."*

important things of life: battle and wenching! O, yes, this plump wife may moan and sigh for him now, but she'll forget him soon enough, you have my word on't! In a week or two she'll be making the beast with two backs with brave Persival, for to tell the truth I do believe that Persival's limpness of member is but a passing affliction. Nay, nay, foolish merchant! Trust not her groans and sighs, her snorts and gasps! Earnest though they be now, she'll play thee false in the end! Ah, but do forgive this outburst, Sir Launcelot. Tis but my bone-deep disgust for all merchants—the blood-sucking, lickshit bastards! But pray continue your fine tale."

"Well, it came to pass that—"

"Not that I have pity for the low merchant, mind! There's two things I cannot abide in this life! One is a merchant, and the other is a cuckold! But enough said. Please continue."

"Ah . . . well, when the merchant did, in a month's time, return—"

"After all, what use is there for merchants' wives, if not to be swiven by passing knights from time to time? What other function have they? To give suckle to more merchants to steal a man's farms and rents from him? Nay, they be as useless as priests that know none but dull edifying tales . . . speaking of which: Wake up, young clerke! If thou canst not contribute to the entertainment, thou canst at least have the decency to attend to it, that thou might con a story or two for future telling. Wake up, I say!"

And the priest gasped and startled up from dreams wherein his pissette had been used by a thousand witches in tug o' war, and in his waking confusion he did grasp down and find it sore enough that the dream might have been true. He sank back all weary in his chair, his arms dangling to his sides and his eyes staring dully ahead, so broken and fatigued was he with his pious exercises of that evening.

Then up spake the fair Elaine. "Good Baron, well know I that the years have somewhat tarnished my beauty, but within I am much the same as in my youth, for it is one of the burdens of age to wither without ere one has ripened within. And even at this moment, as when I was in my maiden years, I feel the need upon me to be shriven of my sins. Thinkest thou that thy priest has holiness and puissance left to attend to the inner needs of one fallen so low as I?"

The priest gawked, stunned and affrighted, muttering, "Ah, nay . . . nay, but . . ."

"Now, now, fair Elaine, hold not thyself in such base esteem," said the Baron generously. "For, though thou hast indeed travelled far down the road towards ugliness, yet thy nobility be shown in the way thou weavest a tale. Maugre thy low condition and seeming haggishness, I am sure the priest would eagerly shrive you—"

"No, wait!" panted the priest. "Listen . . ."

"Yea," continued the Baron, "it is said that all people are equal in the eyes of God—though I confess I did never see the advantage in that. And the good priest here— But hold! Where *be* the priest? Ah, there he is, under the table. Come, come, man! Think not that thou must amuse us with thy pranks in recompense for thy dinner, for we have Sir Launcelot and the fair Elaine to make our entertainment. Off with thee, lad. Take this something used damsel above and shrive her as fully as thou hast shriven my wife and daughter."

The priest crawled from beneath the table and stood to his feet, swaying and all limp, muttering weak protests and shaking his head slowly from side to side. But the fair Elaine offered him words of encouragement as she took him firmly by the arm and led him, whimpering, to the shriving place.

"And now, Sir Launcelot," said the Baron, beaming and rubbing his hands together, "let us have more of this tale of Persival the Rude. Enough of this dallying!"

The old beggar-knight stared at the Baron for a moment, then said, "Art quite sure thou hast done with thy damnable interruptions?"

"Oh, yes. Quite sure."

"Hm-m-m," old Launcelot said uncertainly. "Very well, then." He cleared his throat and struck his bardic pose. "Then was it that Rude Persival found himself—"

"After all," the Baron said, "a man would be a veriest ass to interrupt again and again a tale he lusted to hear."

"Would he?" Launcelot asked coldly.

"Yes, indeed. The flow of the story would be quite broken, don't you see. But enough of all this! On with the tale, man! On with the tale!"

S T A V E VI

IN WHICH PERCY SAVES A SWALLOWED MAN, FALLS
VICTIM TO THE CURSE OF CRONIDD, SURVIVES
THE RITUAL OF ELEVATION AND DISAPPEARANCE,
AND THUS BECOMES A TRUE KNIGHT; THIS
BEING PART THE SECOND:
THE MAKING OF
A KNIGHT.

ld Sir Launcelot took up his tale again,
saying, "And thus it was that Rude Persival found himself bound and beaten,
lying on the floor of the inn, and awaiting his death at the hands of the Swallowed Man. And know ye that—"

"Hold!" cried the Baron. "Bound and beaten? On
an inn floor? A Swallowed Man? Pray examine the
fabric of thy tale well, fellow knight, for I fear it's torn
and some goodly part of thy story has fallen through!"

"In truth, brother knight," the ancient beggar explained, "the tale continued through thy rare irksome
interruptions, and thou hast missed some portions
thereof."

"Nay, say not so! Cannot we turn back and re-
speak the missing bits?"

"Alas, no. For know ye that History makes its

creeping, inexorable voyage from Ago to Anon, and no work of man can pause that fleeting Now. For even in the saying of 'now,' when a man be voicing the O, the N be in the dusty past, and the W yet unborn."

The Baron pondered this concept for a time, then said, "Thou wouldst not shit a fellow knight, I hope."

"Nay, never."

"But tell me this much at least: Did Percy have at the merchant's wife?"

"Often and well."

"Ah-ha! Just as I feared. She and all her false pantings and groans of sadness! And what of the merchant? Did he return?"

"In due course. But, alack the day, he survived his return by only two weeks."

"How can that be? Men may be driven mad by being made cuckold, but never have I known one to die of it."

"'Twas indirectly he died of it."

"O, yes, of course. To be sure. Indirectly. Just as I thought." The Baron nodded sagely. Then he frowned and his eyes flickered back and forth in doubt and confusion. "Ah . . . how exactly does one die indirectly of being horned?"

"Well, know ye that when the plump wife came to know the pleasures of the bed as taught by Persival, she made like demands upon the merchant, and in his feeble attempts to perform, he did one night clutch at his breast, whimper, whinny, and expire."

"Serves the lickshit money-grubber right for gobbling up bits of a man's land! So Persival got all his goods and chattel?"

"Indirectly."

"O, yes! Indirectly again. Ah . . . how?"

"The wife got them, but she gave all freely enough to Persival."

"In exchange for his promise to bung her barrel nightly, I daresay."

"Their compact had those properties."

"But the brave lad got weary of the same old barrel, so off he scarpered, right?"

"I could not myself have limned the event with greater celerity, appreciation of motive, or leanness of style."

The Baron nodded. "Well, breeding will out in the long run, I suppose. All right. So now we have Persival with all the merchant's coin, and the plump wife sobbing on the floor. Begin there, and tell the tale. And the devil's piss on all your N's and W's and O's, for I conned the tale out of you anyway!"

The merchant's coin at his belt, ever dispensed with grand and generous hand, young Persival made threescore days great pleasure and high riot in the inns and taverns, nor was he wanting for friends to aid in the task of merrymaking. Ah, what drinking and feasting there was! What song and laughter!

But alas, pleasure is fragile and fleeting, and life's true fabric has toil in the warp and pain in the woof, so it was inevitable that Percy's joy, too full and too deep, would be of short term. And one morning Percy awoke from a hard night's sleep under the table of a distant rustic inn knowing not where he was or how he came to be there. And when the smarmy inn-keeper presented his reckoning, the young scamp discovered his purse to be as empty as the heart of a whore, or the mind of a priest, or the experience of a scholar. And not only was Percy bereft of coin, but by one of those coincidences that ironic Fate delights in, all his friends of two months had vanished, together with their vows of lasting affection.

Now the inn-keeper was so wroth that the veins did bulge in his neck, but his wife, who had experienced the Flaw during the roistering of that night, spoke calming words, saying, "Nay, husband, rant not so; nor beat the wall in fury; nor tug the last hairs from thy pate in despair. Give over swearing the vengeance of the baillif, and pleading on behalf of thy sickly parents, and throwing thyself on the floor, and begging a rope to hang thy ruined self, and thumping thy forehead on the table, and clawing thy breast, and kicking the dog. These exercises will not grow coin in an empty purse. Show thyself a pitiful Christian and offer to take the lad on to do low and mean tasks in the innyard till his reckoning be satisfied."

As there was nought else for it, the inn-keeper followed the counsel of his wife and permitted young Persival to labour in the innyard from first light to last. Yet oft did the hosteller sigh and aver that the damnable foible of charity in his nature would ruin him in the end. But know you that his ill will was not shared by the wife, nor by their two frick daughters, nor by the scullery wenches, nor by the milkmaid, nor by certain of the lady guests, nor by the prioress of the nearby nunnery, all of whom found opportunities to comfort the lad in his sorrow and toil.

Thus did Percy pass many months in the service of this country inn, toiling by day and plying by night, so that his health did begin to suffer therefrom. But no closer came he to removing himself from bondage, for the inn-keeper reckoned his found and shelter at a trifle more than his wage. And it might have come to pass that Percy's tale would be a brief one, for both his chores and his joys were draining his brawn, had he not blundered upon the adventure known afar and close as The Trial of the Swallowed Knight.

Now, I have sung of Percy's life in Lud's Towne, where he proved himself cunning enough in the slights and crafts of the streets. But he was a town whelp and all ignorant of the nobler aspects of life. Never had he heard of chivalry; never had he thrilled to a tourney; never, indeed, had he so much as seen a knight in armour, and this last gap in his experience came nigh to being his downfall.

Percy was about his work in the innyard when a guest upon a great charger beat on the inn gate and demanded entrance in a loud and gruff voice. Percy looked out through the spyhole, and he was stunned by the wonderous vision that assailed his eyes.

"What's this?" he asked his amazed self. "By the epistolary balls of Paul, tis some poor sod been swallowed whole by an iron monster! I can see his face peeking out from within the metal jaws of the beastly thing! And Percy, who if ignorant was not craven, determined to rescue the swallowed man.

With great stealth, he slipped out through the back gate and approached the Iron Ogre from behind. Then, with a desperate yelp, he leapt up and tugged the monster from his saddle and sat upon its metal chest while he pried open that ghastly iron mouth! Then did he reach down the gullet till his hand felt

the face of the swallowed man! "Take heart, me fellow!" he cried. "Don't give up hope! There! I've got
thee by the nose! Now, out you come!" And he did
tug for all his worth! But the monster would not give
up its dinner without a fight. It kicked and swung its
metal arms, and the more Percy pulled at the nose of
its meal, the more the ogre flailed about and struggled! And to the grunts and curses of the panting
Percy, and the clattering of the wrathful Thing, was
added the howling of the swallowed man, who in his
desperate confusion seemed less than grateful to his
saviour.

All the bruit and shouting brought the inn-keeper
to the gate, a stout cudgel in his fist. And with a cry of
dismay, that worthy rushed into the melee, applying
his club with wonderous vigour.

"Lay off, for God's sake!" cried Percy. "An thou
canst not better aim thy blows to the monster, thou be
more hinderance than help!"

"Desist, fool! Desist!" cried the inn-keeper.

"Nay, master! For see thee not that I have the
poor fellow's head half out through the monster's
mouth, though it entailed some damaging of the
ears?"

At that moment, a great blow from the inn-keeper's cudgel brought the blessings of sleep to the fatigued Percy.

After some lapse of time, the lad awoke through
pain to find himself bound and beaten, lying on the
floor of the inn. And standing over him, scowling and
frowning, was a gentleman whose countenance was
remarkable for the bruising of his nose and a certain
irregularity about the ears. Beside the strange gentle-

man was the inn-keeper, smiling and smarmy, rubbing his hands together, bobbing and bowing.

The stranger prodded Percy with his toe and said,
"What say ye, low inn-keeper, to my trussing up this
scamp to a tree as a target for the exercise of my
lance?"

"An excellent idea, my lord! Right cunning and
nobly contrived. Shall I fetch rope?"

"Nay, now I think on't, I would not besmear my
lance with the gore of this insignificant whelp."

"Ah, true, noble guest. I should have thought of
that myself. Ah! What sayest thou to this? Thou mightest pass a rope about his feet and drag him from the
pommel of thy horse about the village at a gallop. I
know some places of rough cobble and sharp corners
that would make high sport of it."

"Hm-m-m! Thou hast a merry wit, for a scrofulous
fleakson of an inn-keeper."

"O, gramercy, my lord, though I little merit thy
praise. Wouldst accept some wine, perhaps? A joint
well roasted? A scullery wench well scrubbed?"

"Yea, bring on some refreshment; and as I gorge,
I shall consider the fate of this shitten scamp."

The knight took his place at the high table, while
the inn-keeper scurried to his service, cringing to
the gentleman, but roaring abuse at family and hire-
lings.

When Percy had a little regained his wits, he discovered that he was not alone in his discomfort, for
lying beside him, also coiled about with rope in such
wise that he could not scratch the flea that paraded up
and down his nose, was an ancient beggar of uncommon ugliness.

Percy spake in low voice to his companion in misery, asking, "Tell me, Old 'Un, knowest thou what foul thing I have done to be bashed and trussed up so?"

"Foolish lad," croaked the clapperdudgeon, "thou hast made bold to attack yon knight, to drag him from his charger, and to offer considerable insult to his noble nose. These actions were both impetuous on thy part and somewhat irregular by way of greeting a guest to thine inn. I doubt not that thou wilt suffer well for your sins. Would I might witness thy chastisement, for twill be a lively affair of wonderous invention and thoroughness. But, alas, my hours are fewer than thine." And the Old 'Un sobbed, and a tear coursed down his nose, to the annoyance of the flea.

But Percy complained that he remembered offering no insult to this knight of the long nose, and indeed the last memory in his throbbing head was his efforts to save a swallowed man from an iron monster. Then it was that the Old 'Un explained to Percy the nature of armour.

"Nay," protested Percy, "surely thou jesteth. No man of sound mind would go about in a suit of iron. Out upon thy banter! Is his tailor a tinker, then? And how, when a great need to piss is upon him, does he claw out his hose? Nay, Old 'Un! Think me not so great a fool as to believe thee!"

But the Old 'Un persisted in his assertion that yonder knight was both the iron monster and the swallowed man, and in the end he prevailed upon Percy to believe him.

"Yea, but," wondered Percy, "why did my master the inn-keeper belabour *my* head with a stick? It meseemeth that else I would have had the better of this fellow."

"Tis because yon man's a knight, while thou art something less, and not even that for long."

"Yea, but why does the inn-keeper bow low and scrape, while the other sneers at the viands and complains of the wine?"

"Tis because he is a knight."

"Yea, but how dares the man make so free with the inn-keeper's wife and daughters, ever with his hand upon their arses and weighing their bubbies in his palm, while the inn-keeper pretends to examine the ceiling with close attention?"

"Tis because he is a knight."

"Yea, but look you how the inn-keeper offers his reckoning, and the other pushes it aside and threatens to ram it up the old man's cul if it is offered again."

"Tis because he is a knight, I tell you!"

Percy considered all this for a long time, then he said, "I confess in all honesty, Old 'Un, that I do begin to think this trade of knight is the best to follow. Pray, what must a man do to prentice to the craft?"

"I shall explain all, but first I beg thine aid with this irksome flea upon my nose, for know you that it does parade up and down and bite at each turning till the water stands in mine eyes for the very itching of it. Yet I am so bound about by ropes that I can do nought but cross mine eyes to better observe its insults."

"Gladly would I assist thee, Old 'Un, but wot ye not that my arms are wrapped tight to my sides also? Ah! A moment! It occurs to me that my legs are free. I shall study how I may be of service to thee."

With this, rude Percy squirmed and strove until he had wriggled about on the floor and had gained position to deliver the flea a great blow with his boot. And this he did, teaching that flea a lesson it would not soon forget. "There now!" said Percy. "Thou shalt no longer be tormented by that flea, Old 'Un. . . . Old 'Un? Hey-ho! Old 'Un!"

Slowly the ancient prisoner came to his senses. "A thousand thanks, young master," he said groggily. "Mayhaps I shall find a chance to do thee like service."

"Twas my pleasure. Before nodding off, thou hadst promised to tell me what a man must do to become a knight and merit all his privilege. Pray, pursue that."

And so the Old 'Un informed Rude Percy that a knight was required to do noble deeds, amongst which were the Bashing of Ogres, the Rescuing of Maidens and Subsequent Swiving Thereof, the Slaying of Saracens, the Spurning of Common People, the Cheating of Merchants, the Questing for Holy Grails—

"For *what?*" asked Percy, laughing.

"Nay, ask me not what a grail be, young master. Tis a profound mystery, and properly so. For much of the honour that accrues to the questing is in the sore difficulty of seeking that of which one knows nothing. But beyond these common tasks and deeds of a knight must be a willingness to offer combat to any passing knight who is in a brave or feisty mood. But know you that these adventures may not be undertaken by one who is unknighted. For if a common man were to bash

and kill and wench, then he is accounted an outlaw
and a brigand. It is not so much *what* one does, it is
largely a matter of style." And he went on to say that
he knew all about such things because, in his youth,
he had been a lower servant in a noble house. "And
know ye, young master, that being kicked and cuffed
by the nobility is an edifying and enriching experience; while being kicked and cuffed by common people is little better than a nuisance."

Percy's eyes glowed with interest, for know you
that he had quite decided to give up being a yard boy
at an inn in favour of being a knight, for this trade
seemed to have rather more to recommend it. "But
how does one go about being knighted, Old 'Un?"

"Hast a wife, and couldst play the pliant husband
whilst the king swived her?"

"Alas, no."

"Hm-m-m. Well, hast money to lend to a king?"

"Alas, no."

"Hm-m-m. Well, canst ride a horse to the winning
of races?"

"Again, no. And again, alas."

"Hm-m-m. Canst sing so loudly that fame and
wealth be brought to the nation?"

"No again. To say nothing of alas."

"Ah, then," the Old 'Un sighed and shook his
head. "Thou has no course other than the proving of
thy valour."

"In what manner?"

"By offering combat to passing knights, of course.
How else? But think not to amble up to the nearest
knight and offer to knock him upon his arse. Nay, nay.

An thou be not well caparisoned in armour and mounted upon a noble steed, no worthy knight would deign to do battle with thee."

"And how would I gain an iron suit and a stout mount?"

"Why, by being a knight, of course!"

Percy pondered this a moment. "If I comprehend thee rightly, one must be a knight ere he can become a knight."

"Aye, thou hast it. But all this parleevoo is but dream stuff and fragile, for thou art like to be crow-meat before dawn in just punishment for the insult thou didst offer to yon knight. And, what is worse, I am like to precede thee to Purgatory." And with this the Old 'Un sighed right piteously.

"But what hast thou done to merit this harsh fate? Hast thou also offered to snatch a swallowed man from the jaws of an iron ogre?"

"Nay, young master. I be not such an ass as thee. My sin lies in the fact that I am the Giant Monster of the Grail."

"Thou?"

"Yea, even I."

"But thou art something scrawny for a giant, Old 'Un, though I confess thee ugly enough to be a monster, if I may say so without offence."

"In truth, young master, I did not ken myself to be a giant monster till I was edified in this regard by yon knight. I was this morning wandering the road in search of shelter, when I was of a sudden accosted by this knight, who prodded at my breeches with his lance and called out, 'Give over, baleful Giant Monster of the Grail! Thou art rendered prisoner unto me!'

On hearing this, I did look about to see the monster
so addressed. But as we were alone upon that road, all
logick did suggest that I be the target of these brave
words. Then did I pluck the lance away from mine
arse and speak humbly to the noble gentleman, assur-
ing him that I was not a giant monster, nor had I any
aspirations in that direction. But the good knight
averred firmly that he knew me to be a cruel and re-
sourceful monster possessing the power to change my
appearance to that of a low, whining, somewhat ugly
beggar with a hole in his breeches. And he went on to
say that he would gain honour and repute through the
slaying of me. So it was that he trussed me up and
brought me hence that he might have witnesses to his
brave slaying of the Giant Monster of the Grail. And
know you that I was sore fatigued when we arrived at
the inn gate, for he trotted his horse all the way, and I
had to run along before him quite gamely for my age
and stiffness of limb, for the point of his lance hovered
ever but inches from mine arse."

At this moment Percy's attention was drawn from
the Old 'Un's tale by an angry roar issuing from the
knight, who, having drunk long and well of the wine
he despised as beneath his tastes, had come in his
befuddlement to the belief that the inn-keeper was
the Ogre of the Grail, in which guise he was the natural recipient of the curses and blows of any Christian
knight. With dim but vicious eye, he advanced upon
that cringing inn-keeper, dagger in hand, while the
other retreated, quaking and babbling piteous asser-
tions that he was no ogre and had not seen a grail for
years. But the knight was not to be tricked by such
transparent ruses as these, and with slow determined

prowl he moved in upon his prey, which prey fell to its knees and clasped its hands in whimpering supplication, all the while shuffling away on its knees with stiff little steps. The knight made a bold lunge with his dagger, and with a yelp the inn-keeper leapt to his feet and jumped back with such good will that he retreated into the hearth wherein great logs did burn merrily. A tongue of flame licked at his fud, causing him such surprise and pain that he did scream and bolt forward, quite upsetting the drunken knight, who fell back, cracking his head first upon the corner of the table, then upon the edge of the stool, then upon the floor, the fatigues of which exercise were such that he chose to rest in deep sleep before continuing the battle.

Then did the wife rush in crying, "What hast thou done, husband and stupid shitport? Think ye to brutalise a knight without punishment? O, woe upon our house!" And she did wring her hands and weep and cry calamity. But for a time the inn-keeper did not concern himself with the dire outcome of his rash action, for he was closely occupied with slapping his arse, that he might somewhat diminish the fire which smouldered there, all the while hopping about with an agility wonderous in a man of his girth and years.

The two daughters of the family did rush in and contribute right willingly to the bruit and confusion, one falling in a swoon upon her mother, and the other seeking to assist the father by applying a broom to his arse with such good will that her zeal quite exceeded the period of need, which the inn-keeper seemed to resent, for once the smoulder upon his arse was beaten out, he snatched the broom from his daughter and served her with like blows.

"What, mad fiend?" screeched the wife. "Having damaged yon knight and guest, is the taste for blood so upon thee that thou wouldst carry havoc even to thine own flesh? Have this for thine improvement, then!" With this, she took up a great skillet and applied it right smartly and often to the inn-keeper's back. Now it came to pass that in her chasing of the inn-keeper to firk him with skillet, as he was chasing his daughter to firk her with the broom, the wife left her swooning daughter bereft of support and the girl fell, sitting with great force upon the face of the fallen knight, whose already swollen nose did in this way receive some further insult. Now, the scampering daughter did happen to trip over the seated one, and the father over her, and the mother over him, and for a time they made a fine tangle of flailing arms and legs with fists and feet working blind damage upon whatever came their way. And know you that the face of the sleeping knight did receive considerable attention. But fatigue at last overcomes even the gayest sport, and in the fulness of time the flaying and cuffing and kicking was replaced by panting and wheezing, and each person did contrive to untangle his members from those of the others, save for the knight, who slept on, little wotting that, although he had taken no active part in the combat, his face had been the very battle-field of it.

Now, it was not long before the wife fell to considering what vengeance the knight might wreak, when he returned to his senses, and she pondered how to avoid the punishment that would surely befall them. In the durance, the inn-keeper took this opportunity to pay himself his reckoning from the fallen knight's purse. Then it occurred to him that it might be an act of wise foresight to pay the bill of the next knight who might happen by. And why not a third? And when he had compensated himself for these future losses, he noted that the paltry sum remaining in the purse was something of an insult to the owner, so he took this as well.

Now know ye that Rude Percy and the Old 'Un had not failed to observe these vigourous happenings, trussed up as they were and with nothing else to occupy their attention. Then did the Old 'Un speak up, crying, "O misfortune! O calamity! O havoc! O shit!"

The inn-keeper's wife snarled at the Old 'Un, asking what right *he* had to complain so.

But the Old 'Un wagged his head and answered, "Nay, lady! Think not that I be such a fool. For I can read the sly intent that even now is taking root in thy mind. Well know I that thou plottest to cut the bonds of myself and my young friend here and urge us to flee. O, woe!"

"Why would I do so giddy a thing as that?" demanded the wife.

"Nay, give over this feigning, lady. For I can see that thou dost complot to free us into the night that thou mightest excuse thyself to yon felled knight when, befuddled with wine and firking, he comes again to his senses. For thou dost connive to tell him that the two of us did succeed in loosening our bonds and did fall upon him whilst he was in his cups, and did bash and firk him smartly and often, then did take the coin from his purse, then did cowardly flee. And thou shalt seem guiltless, while we shall be outlaws condemned to the forests and byways. O! mischance! O! shit!"

Now the inn-keeper and the wife did fall into close parley, their foreheads touching and their voices low, and now and again they did look up at the fallen knight and the bound prisoners, and they did chuckle together.

When they had made an end to these sly councils, the inn-keeper yode him to where Percy and the Old 'Un were bound. Smiling and rubbing his hands together, he said, "My good wife and I have consulted our consciences and found therein a Christian impulse. Since yon fallen knight's wrath will be full and ultimate over his firking at our hands, and as we can suffer no more for your freedom than we shall suffer for his pains, we have decided to exercise charity on your behalf. For he is mean and low who avoids such kindness as costs him nothing. And do not fear that our intent is to set the blame for the knight's bashing upon your shoulders. A curse be on the lickshit slanderer who would say so!" And with this he did take up a knife and cut the bonds of the two.

"Let us be off at once!" said Percy.

But the Old 'Un sat chafing the blood back into his limbs and saying to the inn-keeper, "Again I can read thy sly intent. Thou art considering that it would not do for us to be found and captured soon, as our stories of the firking might be at some contradiction to thine. And so, to give us the strength that hot flight

requires, thou art even now plotting to foist a rich
repast upon us. Ah, inn-keeper," he said wagging a
finger at him, "thou art cunning indeed."

"Hm-m-m," said the inn-keeper. Then he gave
instructions to his daughters, who scurried to the scullery.

Percy and the Old 'Un waged great combat
amongst the viands set before them, the ancient beggar showing himself a trencherman of no small accom-
plishment, as he did consume somewhat more than
he did weigh.

But the wife spake urgently to them, saying,
"Make haste with your gorging, pray, and begone. For
even now yon knight does make small moans and
movements!"

And true it was that the fallen knight did seem to
regain some part of his senses, for he did groan and
all groggily set his fingers tenderly to his swollen face
and mutter, "Methinks I have been firked."

The Old 'Un sat back from his feast, his fingers
twined behind his head and a broom straw between
his teeth. "Bring forth a bowl of wine, my good man.
And as for the knight, take my counsel. Firk him further, and later set it to our account."

Now the inn-keeper was well exercised in the
practice of setting the uses of one to the account of
another, so right willingly did he take up his cudgel
and apply it first to one side of the knight's head, then
to the other, in such a wise that the noble gentleman
returned to that deep repose that is sovereign physick
for sagging health.

When, in his own good time, the Old 'Un had
done with the feasting and drinking, he sucked his

fingers clean and belched in deep contentment, then he rose and bade Percy collect such things as belonged to him, that they might commit themselves to the road ere dawn found them out.

"Truly, Old 'Un, I have but small treasure about me, and that be in the cow shed. I shall gather it as we pass."

"Ah, young master? And what nature of small treasure be it?"

Percy shrugged. "Tis but a few silver coins given me by the local prioress for the servicing of her and the maintenance of the secret."

And with the mention of silver coins, the Old 'Un's eyes twitched and darted as he studied how to relieve his young companion of this barrier to heaven.

So it was that the young scapegrace and the old scoundrel did make their leave. And know you that, for all their eagerness to have him carry away the guilt and blame for the firking of the knight, yet was there some regret in the hearts of the wife, the daughters, and the girls of the scullery, for they knew they would not experience the like of Rude Percy's Flaw again in this life, although they might in heaven, if that reward be all it was bruited to be.

For a season, Rude Percy and the Old 'Un wandered the roads by night and sought secret haven in the forests by day. For know you that they dared not walk upon the public way openly, for in every village and hamlet they heard rumour of an angry knight, long of nose and bruised of face, who was scouring the land in search of two villains of description not far from their own.

One bright afternoon when they were resting in a

copse, Percy did offer to show his small cache of treasure to the Old 'Un, who had by inadvertence brought the talk around to the general subject of such silver coins as were given by prioresses to yard boys for servicing them and maintaining the secret. The Old 'Un tugged open the purse and peered within. Then, of a sudden, he threw the purse from him with a scream and scrubbed his fingers on his blouse. "Nay, nay, young friend! I cannot touch those coins! Though I like thee well enough, yet I dare not share the calamity that sits upon thy shoulders!"

"Of what calamity dost thou rave, Old 'Un?"

But the beggar waggled his head, set his finger beside his nose, and grinned sagely. "Nay, think not to con me with this pretence of innocence. Thou knowest well enough that these be the very coins of Gwillibedd, which disks of evil silver carry with them the Curse of Cronidd!"

"The Curse of Cronidd?" Percy asked, astonished and frozen in the very act of picking up the purse, which now he durst not touch.

"Feign not ignorance, young scamp, nor essay to pretend that thou hast never heard of the Curse of Cronidd."

"By the saline balls of Lot's wife, I swear I know not whereof thou speakest, Old 'Un!"

"Hm-m-m. Perchance thou feignest not. Perchance thou wert tricked in this matter by the prioress that gave thee the coins. Ah, treacherous nonne, to have served thee with such guile!"

"But tell me, of what consists this Curse of . . . of what?"

"Cronidd. All men, learned and lewd, know that

*"THOU KNOWEST WELL ENOUGH THAT THESE BE THE VERY COINS OF GWILLIBEDD,
WHICH DISKS OF EVIL SILVER CARRY WITH THEM THE CURSE OF CRONIDD!"*

he who possesses these damned coins will be cursed with Despair, Death, Damnation, and Flatulence—a curse that can be escaped only by the performance of *the Ritual.*"

Young Percy gnashed his teeth and beat his hands against his head and complained to God that this misfortune should befall him. And roundly did he grieve to have fallen victim to the Curse of . . .

". . . what was it called again?"

"Cronidd, damn it! Cronidd!"

"Ah yes, Cronidd. Ah, woe! That this should come to me, who have done ill to no man and service to every woman!"

"Yea, tis rare sad, young friend. And I do lament on thy behalf. By the bye, did I forget to mention . . . *the Ritual?*"

"Ritual? What ritual?"

"The ritual by which thou mightest escape the consequences of the Curse, of course." And so saying, the Old 'Un fixed his attention on a cloud passing overhead and whistled between his teeth, demonstrating that he had no further interest in this light parley.

But Persival grasped his tattered jerkin and said, "Tell me of the Ritual, for pity's sake!"

"Of what?" asked the Old 'Un with a vague expression.

"The Ritual!"

"Oh, yes. The Ritual. Ah, tis nought but an ancient and unholy rite thou mightest perform to set thee to lee of the vengeance of the Curse of Cronidd. Nothing more. Not worth mentioning." And with this the Old 'Un laid back upon the sward, crossed his ankle upon his knee, linked his fingers behind his head, and reposed himself for a nap with several smackings of his lips.

But frantic Percy was of a different mind. He lifted open the eyelids of the Old 'Un with his fingers and shouted down upon him, "Sayest thou there be a rite by which I could avert my fate?"

"Yea, e'en so. But alas, it is not a rite thou canst perform." And with this the Old 'Un pushed away Percy's fingers and closed his eyes again.

"What is the use of a rite I cannot perform? Tis useless as a frog's fart which, being loosed under water, doth give away his hiding place and, though it bring him some temporary relief, doth make him victim to those who would prey upon him! Tis as useless as that!"

"There is something of the poet in thee, young friend," the Old 'Un said sleepily, "and something of the philosopher too. But know that when I said that thou canst not perform the rite, I meant that thou canst not perform it *alone*. For know ye that the Ritual must be performed by *two* men. And few are they who would assist thee in the performing of it, for it involves calling down the forces of darkness and endangering both soul and body. You see . . . the Ritual involves both Elevation and Disappearance, as such rituals commonly do."

Persival's mind was all fear and confusion, and he demanded to know the meaning of this Elevation and Disappearance.

The Old 'Un drew a long sigh and sat up, complaining that he was like to have no rest till he impart his knowledge. Then he described the Ritual thus:

To avoid the Curse of Cronidd, two men must say together silent magic incantations. Then must they dig a shallow hole and bury the coins, after which they must sleep through the night. And when dawn comes, one of them will be blessed with Elevation, much to be envied; but the other will be cursed with Disappearance, much to be dreaded.

"Aye," said Persival, "but what be an Elevation, and what be a Disappearance?"

"Oh, an Elevation be an Elevation of the common sort, the raising of a base and lowborn man to the state of knighthood, such as thou wert envying after on the inn floor some space of time ago."

"Ah, and what be a Disappearance?"

"Oh, a Disappearance be a Disappearance of the common sort, in which the other performer of the rite will vanish, together with the cursed coins. And it is the mere whim of fate that dictates which of the two will be blessed by Elevation and which condemned to Disappearance. But alas, young friend, where could you find a man so foolish as to perform the Ritual with thee? For although Elevation to impoverished knighthood is a goal devoutly to be sought, yet only a fool would risk being damned to Disappearance together with the cursed coins." And with this the Old 'Un sighed compassionately and lay back to rest upon the sward.

For some time, Percy mulled and sifted these matters in his mind. Then slowly a cunning ploy took shape in his imagination.

"Ah . . . Old 'Un?" he began, as offhandedly as possible.

"Hm-m-m?"

"I have a thought."

"Hast?"

"See here, Old 'Un. Consider thine estate. Thou art lowly, feeble, hungry, flea-bit, ugly of face, shitten of garment, and stunning of smell. Be honest and straight and confess it."

"Yea, tis true. Tis true," the Old 'Un said thoughtfully.

"Now consider this. If thou shouldst participate with me in the Ritual, and if it be thy good fortune to be Elevated to the rank of impoverished knight, then thou hast gained much in station and pride."

"Yea, tis true. Tis true."

"And if, through unlikely misfortune, thy lot should be the curse of Disappearance, thou hast not lost all that much, considering the miserable thing thou art."

"Yea, tis true. Tis true."

"Thou hast much to gain, with but little risk."

"Hm-m-m." And for some time the Old 'Un pondered this proposal. At last he sat up, smiled upon the lad, and grasped his hand, saying, "By God, I will perform the Ritual with thee, young friend! But think not that thou hast gulled me with thy honey'd persuasion. Nay, rather it is our friendship that brings me to this generous decision."

Tears of gratitude stood in Persival's eyes as he wrung the Old 'Un's hand. "Now what sayest thou? Let us be to the Ritual! Thou hast said that first we must kneel together and utter silent incantations. I confess that I know not the words of these incantations."

"Fear not. As they are silent, small errors and lesings will pass unnoticed."

For a time they knelt together in intense and earnest silence. Then they scooped out a shallow hole
wherein they dropt the purse of cursed coins. And
having so done, they returned to the shade of their
copse and sought slumber. But sleep came not readily
to young Persival, for he was sore a-throb to know
whether, when he awoke, he would be Elevated or
Disappeared. Night fell, and in course sleep visited
Persival's eyes, and with it came dreams, both gentle
and gnarled. For at one time he would dream himself
risen to the state of impoverished knight, all clad in
iron and grovelled to by inn-keepers. But in the next
wisp of dream stuff, he would find himself in a throng
of women of wonderous beauty, all ignoring him, as
he was Disappeared and not noteworthy. And when
he essayed to drink a bowl of wine, his thirst went
unslaked, for the wine spilled to the ground beneath
him, passing quite through his Disappeared throat.

So it was that with a burning thirst he sprang suddenly to wakefulness and sat up, blinking at the new-
born dawn. For a time, he durst not look at his hands,
lest there be nought at the end of his sleeve. But at
last he forced himself to a trial to learn if he be visible
and whole. Shutting tight his eyes and making his
hardest fist, he delivered to his cheek a great blow to
learn if cheek and fist be substantial.

When he came to his senses, he knew that the
Ritual had worked its miracle, for he discovered that
the Old 'Un and the accursed coins had Disappeared.

For some hours he knelt in the shade of a tree and
prayed for the vanished soul of his old friend. Yet he

soothed his conscience with the knowledge that they had gambled together fairly and that, had Fate been so inclined, it might have been the Old 'Un who knelt here, an impoverished knight, while Persival had vanished with the coins.

The praying done, Rude Percy—or Sir Persival the Rude, as now he must be styled—tested and exercised his newfound nobility. First he brake off a twig from a tree and, holding it to his side, he strode back and forth, turning of a sudden and brandishing his twig when some caitiff bush did offer him insult or challenge. Then did he attack the bush with brave strokes and bold and prove his valour upon it. Then did he practise holding his chin high and looking at things about him as though they stank and were filthy, and he made his nostrils to quiver and his lips to curl. Then he tried his voice in harsh commands and snide asides. And know you that he was convinced by the swagger of his walk and the snarl of his voice that the Ritual had indeed worked its magic and elevated him to noble, if impoverished, knighthood.

And he set his thoughts to the gaining of armour and a horse, with which he might ride out in search of brave combat and glory.

And I shall speak of these adventures, directly I have dampened my dusty throat with a bowl of wine.

"A quaint enough tale, I warrant," the Baron said, "but one that verges upon sedition, I vow. Tis a dangerous tale to tell, good Sir Launcelot. The values of society and the ways of God are questioned grievously when we are asked to laugh at a firked and cheated knight. Ah, but look ye, here comes the ancient crone who is in fact the fair Elaine, returning from her shriving! And I discern that the lifting of sin from her soul has done her much good, for see how she skips and grins, though her newfound purity has little affected her rare and wonderous ugliness, which still shines forth in full potency. Come, sit to table, fair Elaine! But tell me, how comes it that the young priest is not with thee?"

"As to that, good mine host, even as he was pressing his efforts to the task of shriving me, that pious man did profess himself too spent with relieving the burdens of sin to return to table, and he did moan and whimper and beg leave to rest a term before rejoining our company."

The Baron shook his head sadly. "I fear this younger crop of priests does lack the zeal and puissance of their predecessors, who could shrive a whole parish before dinner and still have force left to pass the night in gorging and drinking and telling fine tales. This weakness is a flaw in their calling. And, speaking of flaws, do let us pursue the tale of Persival and see what wonders he works amongst women with the wielding of his famed Flaw, Sir Launcelot. Hohey! Sir Launcelot! Art fallen asleep over thy wine bowl? Awake! Open thine eyes!"

"Nay, good host," pled the fair Elaine. "Let the fellow rest his invention, for the night be waning and with the dawn we two must be again upon that road to which we are condemned by our enchantment."

"Yea, but does this mean that I must go without tales to amuse my mind? And what of my wife and daughter here, they who frown and scowl at thee for

no reason I can fathom? Are they to lack entertainment?"

"An thou wilt," said the whilom hag. "I shall confect a tale for thee till Launcelot returns from the
gentle world of sleep."

"Ah, good! And dost thou know the third part of
the wonderous tale of Sir Persival and his Flaw? We
have had the Beginning and the Middle, but we are
Endless."

"Alas, I know not that tale. But there is a history
of rare beauty and cunning I have for thee."

"Good. On with it!"

S T A V E VII

IN WHICH SIR GERVAIS IS ENSNARED IN A DIRE

ENCHANTED FOREST WHERE ALL THINGS ARE

OTHER-SEEMING, AND HOW HE CAME TO

EARN THE TITLE: BRASTER OF

ANCIENTS AND SWIVER

OF CRONES.

raster of ancients?" asked the Baron. "Swiver of Crones? But where is the glory in bashing old men? And what joy is there in swiving crones?—no offence intended. How came the brave Sir Gervais to the unmanly forms of the one and the dire drudgery of the other?"

"In following wise . . ."

Upon a soft and fog-laden morning in autumn the bold Sir Gervais rode forth from Camelot in quest of adventure, glory, and such encounters as might enhance his reputation and purse. Soon he found himself deep in a forest where his stallion's hoof made no sound upon the thick matting of leaves as it glid forward past ghosts of trees that emerged from the mists before and vanished into the mists behind. No forest creature stirred; no wind. And overhanging boughs did brush Sir Gervais's armour and hiss upon his helm, the plumes of which drooped limp with damp.

Now, know you that Sir Gervais was a brave man of high blood, so it was only to seek out the foe that his eyes darted from side to side, and it was only to pass the time that he whistled softly, and it was only an itch to grasp his sword in noble combat that sweated his palms, and it was only to seek greater adventure elsewhere that he decided to turn his horse and quit that dark, dank forest.

And the yelp that escaped from his throat had something of the quality of a war cry, when he suddenly espied beside the path a bent and ancient crone of passing laidliness. She stood in silence and beckoned to him with the crooking of a gnarled finger.

His voice tight in his throat, Sir Gervais addressed the hag. "How now, beckoning crone of passing laidliness, canst direct me through this forest? I wit thee rare gifted in the art of telling directions, one of thine eyes scanning to the left whilst t'other scans to the right in such wise that their paths do intersect some few inches before thy hooked nose."

The crone did cackle and turn her face aside modestly. "Nay, good knight, think not to soften the barriers of my chastity with thy cozening praise, for I do suspect that thou hast penetrated the mysteries of this enchanted forest."

"Say what?"

"Nay, feign not, I pray thee Well thou knowest that this is an enchanted forest in which all things appear to be the very opposite of what they are."

"How's that?"

"Nay, nay. Do not pretend ignorance."

And Sir Gervais stood stiff in the saddle with wounded pride. "Thou dost accuse me false, rank hag. Ignorance is no pretence in me, in troth."

"Know ye, good knight, that even my senses are bemused, though I have long lived here. Did I not know the otherwise-seeming enchantment of this place, I would have been astonished to see a scrawny man, all nude and nobby, astride a pig, his knees scrubbing the muddy track, and his feet dangling behind."

The proud knight looked about to discover the person thus limned.

"Tis of thee I speak, fair, yet seeming-ugly, knight."

"Art thou plotting to have thy head bashed in, ugly and seeming-ugly hag, in the hope that such a bashing might work improvement on thine appearance?"

"Nay, stay and be informed. What I have described is only thine image to me and to all others who espy thee in this forest where all things do seem the opposite of what they are. And seeing thee ugly, deformed, puny, and graceless, I know from this evidence that thou art a knight brave, puissant, fair of visage, and nobly mounted."

"Damme, if thou hast not charactered me to the last jot!"

"And I have no doubt, good warrior, that my beauty, grace, delicacy, and blushing youth have, to thee, some other appearance."

"Hast indeed! O, hast indeed!"

The crone—or seeming crone—hearing this did draw a great and shuddering sigh, and a tear worked its way along the valleys and pits of her nose. This tortuous passage gave Sir Gervais season to ponder what had befallen him in this forest of enchantment, and he did conclude that here before him was a deserving target for his amorous combat, as his rank and title gave him particular claim to wayside beauties, just as God had designated the old and fat amongst womanhood as apt things for varlets and husbandmen to roil amongst.

For know you that Sir Gervais was a man of pride in his station, and he would not be denied the appurtenances of his rank, though they be onerous. Thus, though his senses staggered at the ugliness of the crone, his dignity lusted for her.

"Ah, but I forget form and duty," the seeming hag did say. "Surely thou art weary from thine adventures, and I must share the comforts of my castle with thee."

"Thou art gracious . . . fair maiden."

"Princess, actually."

"Forgive me, Princess. May I offer thee to ride behind me?"

"Gladly would I, though I have never before sat astride a pig."

"A pig?"

"Ah, what am I saying? Even I do sometimes err and accept the evidence of mine eyes, though I know better."

And with this the seeming crone grappled up behind Sir Gervais, hitching her skirts high and wrapping her seeming scrawny legs about his.

As they rode forward, Sir Gervais did exercise his courtly speech and praise her, saying, "Knowing that all things here are the reverse of what they seem, fair

Princess, I trow that thou must be a rare beauteous-smelling bit, and that the bouquet rising from thee—this seeming miasma—is in fact essence of spices rare."

The maiden blushed as she wrapped herself closer to him, and his eyes did smart with the beauty of it all.

Not far along, they came to a branch lane leading to a sluggish stream beyond which a crude hovel sagged upon its rough-hewn beams.

The maiden laughed a seeming cackle and said, "See how, as in anticipation of thee, the drawbridge is down in greeting?"

"How sayest thou? Ah! Of course! Know ye that upon first glance I mistook the drawbridge for a slippery log dropt across a sluggish stream." And Sir Gervais did laugh at his error.

It soon became evident that horses, no less than men, were victims of the forest's enchantment, for in the crossing the brave steed slipped from the wide drawbridge as though it had been a narrow log, and the fall precipitated the riders into the moat, out of which they clawed, and beside which Sir Gervais stood at last, the stenchy water draining from his armour.

"I fear thou wilt attrap thy death of cold," the maiden said. "Quickly into the castle and out of that damp armour. A good roasting before the vast hearth will regain thy temper."

And soon the knight stood beneath the soaring vaults of the great hall that had something the appearance of a low and filthy chamber with dirt floor below and oozing rotten thatch above. He shivered, all nude, before the roaring hearth that had rather the aspect of a feeble stick fire the smoke of which pretended to fill the room in its search for chinks and gaps.

Now know you that the maiden had, for the good of her health, doff'd her sodden garments and now stood before him clothed with the economy of Eve.

"My God!" the knight cried. "How beautiful thou must, in reality, be! For if each perfection doth appear a blemish, then thou art Beauty itself, from thy balding pate to thy gnarled toes! I can no longer contain my ardour! Have at, then!"

And for some time, and with much invention, did they tangle and roil in the seeming sodden rushes of the great hall's floor, now as the two-backed beast, now in the posture of dogs, and again with nose to belly. Exhausted at last, and empty of the essence of love, Sir Gervais rolled aside, panting and clutching for a rag to cover his shivering nudity withal, while the maiden (seeming hag) crooned and sighed her affection and strove in many coy and clever ways to rearm him for the battle of love.

For a year and a day, Sir Gervais languished in this enchanted castle, his body nourished by joints of stag that had all the appearance and taste of gruel, and his love nourished by an inner vision too strong to be contradicted by the evidence of his senses. And in this, he was not unlike other men who pass their lives in other forests of enchantment.

Through all this durance, Sir Gervais was in dire struggle with himself, repelled from the princess by the urgings of his senses, and drawn to her by the urgings of his dignity and sense of self-worth. For the appearance of the hag did inflame his loins somewhat

*"THE MAIDEN BLUSHED AS SHE WRAPPED HERSELF CLOSER TO HIM,
AND HIS EYES DID SMART WITH THE BEAUTY OF IT ALL."*

less than does wading in an icy stream, but the knowl-edge of her hidden beauty and high rank heated his blood beyond containment. So it was that, with the play of cooling and heating ever upon him, he grew thin and tetchy and was ever pained with stones in his sack, to the relief of which he did often carry upon his shoulders a great boulder under which weight he did stagger and pant.

Upon the day after the year and a day, the seem-ing crone bade Sir Gervais to offer some proof of his love and go forth against her close enemy, a neigh-bour baron whose oak patch her swine did envy to snout within.

At first, Sir Gervais was loth to do hurt to a knight he had never exchanged courtesies or insults with, but when the seeming hag described the evil baron as a man of many years and frail body, the knight remem-bered his debt for the kindness of his hostess and his duties to chivalry. Thus, after another discomforting mishap upon the drawbridge, he rode forth to avenge all insults, the princess clinging to his back.

Upon the way, they encountered a woodcutter of great girth whose stature was such that he looked eye to eye at the knight, although the one was astride his charger and the other stood upon the ground. Though the peasant's beard was gray, he was firm and sturdy as an oak, and so broad of chest that he, in rough cloth, was fuller and wider than the knight in his metal.

"Tell me, vast varlet," Sir Gervais called out, "knowest thou the hiding place of the evil baron who has given insult to this dainty maiden behind me?"

"Dainty maiden?" laughed the woodcutter.

And the seeming hag whispered in Sir Gervais's

ear hole that he who stood before him, blocking out the sun, was the very baron they sought.

The knight spake behind his hand, asking, "But lacks he not some of the frailty and decrepitude thou hast ascribed to the Baron?"

"Ah, my love, hast thou forgot that all things here are other-seeming?"

"Ah! Of course! But thou art sure yonder giant aroar with laughter is in truth but a puny and feeble thing?"

"Seems he not otherwise?"

"Most otherwise," the knight confessed with an uneasy glance at the giant.

"There thou hast the proof!"

Sir Gervais struggled with the understanding of this for a longish time, then he said, "Ah! Of course!" Whereupon he directed his voice and attention to the seeming giant and said, "Leave off thy laughing, cur! And hear my demands! Grant this princess of passing beauty the use of thine oak patch for the snouting of her swine, or risk a passage at arms with me, Gervais, knight and fellow of the Table Round!"

"Hast taken leave of thy senses, lad? Were we to grapple in anger, I would doubtless bend and crumple thine iron suit in my hands in such wise that thou within must know some passing discomfort."

Sir Gervais whispered over his shoulder to the seeming crone, "How is it that he trembles not at my rank and prowess?"

"Tis clear as a maiden's soul, my lover. Just as he appears to thee to be a vast and well-proportioned man, so dost thou appear to him to be a scrawny thing of slight power."

Sir Gervais blinked for a moment, then, bending his mind to understanding, he cried out, "Ah! Of course!" Then he chuckled to himself. "What a painful surprise it will be for him, should we meet in combat and he learn of his error." Then to the peasant giant he shouted, "Enough of this parley! Do as I bid, or thy brittle old bones be brast by this hand!"

"Nay, child, nay," the seeming giant bellowed. "Do not require that I bash thee. For I am as gentle of humour as I am stout of limb. Know ye that yon stenchy hag has ere now sent bemused fools to take my oak patch from me, and each of those fellows earned damage of woeful kind. But I had rather deal with thee than dent thee. Let us make a bargain. Forsake that crone behind thee and let me welcome thee as a son. For know ye that my daughter is still a maiden, though she be of runting age and lusty temper. But there are no other men in this damned forest than we two." And with this the peasant gestured to the side of the path, where stood a maiden ripe and moist, with breasts that threatened the fabric of her bodice, hair fresh-spun of gold, fair and soft of face, clear of eye, slim of waist, comfortable of haunch, and whose pink tongue did flicker between even teeth of purest white.

The pulse did quop in Sir Gervais's temple. And elsewhere the restraints of his armour did irk him.

But before he could cry "Done!" the seeming hag rasped in his ear, "I note, brave hero, that thou dost pant and drool and bulge and quop, but remember that in this forest all things are other-seeming. This maiden is the very lees and slag of womanhood, ugly beneath description, diseased to marrow, and rare repulsive to unenchanted eyes." And she went on to confide that the source of her discord with the scrawny baron was his hatred of her because he could not marry off his flawed and blemished daughter so long as his neighbour's beauty diminished her by comparison.

After a very long and troubled silence, Sir Gervais said, "Ah! Of course!" But he did breathe a sigh of regret nevertheless. "Without thy guidance, Princess, I might have fallen victim to this knave's plot. The sly bastard! That's it, then!" he cried. "Have at, varlet!"

And with this, he drew out his sword and offered to cleave the woodcutter's pate down to his very grin.

But the seeming giant grasped the steel in midair and snatched it away, brasting it in twain over his knee and tossing the bits into the brook.

"O-o-o, *now* hast thou precipitated my wrath upon thine aged and brittle back!" cried Sir Gervais, and with this he leapt from the saddle and clutched at the seeming giant's throat.

But the woodcutter lifted the hands away as easily as if they had been there in caress, and he slapped the steel gauntlets together again and again until the knight's palms stung with the pain of such applause. Then the varlet turned the knight upside down and shook him until his head was the clapper in the bell of his helm.

"There, now," the woodcutter said, setting Sir Gervais again upon his feet. "Let that be an end to it. If thou wilt not have my daughter to wed, so be it. Go now and harry me no further."

Dazed, the knight reeled to his horse and clung panting to the stirrup.

The seeming hag leaned down and whispered to him, "Pray be more gentle with the old fool. While I would fain see him punished for his insults, I would not have the sin of murder upon thy soul."

"Say what?" Sir Gervais muttered, half senseless.

"Thou hast done him telling hurt, and I doubt not that he will yield himself after another such chastisement."

"Art sure I have wrought hurt upon him?"

"Joy o' my nights, hast forgot that all things here are other-seeming?"

"Hm-m-m." The battered knight frowned in deep thought. "Un-n-n-h." He squinted at the sky in concentration. "Ah-h-h-h." He squeezed his eyes shut and marshalled all his reasoning powers against the problem. "Oh-h-h. Ah! Of course!" And with this he flung himself again at the seeming giant's throat.

Annoyed by the knight's persistence, the woodcutter grasped him by his ankles and used him as a bludgeon to punish some of the stouter trees until, weary with this pastime, he forced the helmet into the fork of an oak and left Sir Gervais hanging by his chin, swaying gently in the breeze. And with this he strode off, taking his seeming frick and moist daughter with him.

With a sigh and a shake of the head and a toss of the fig, the seeming hag forsook the knight as useless in the gaining of snouting rights in the oak patch, and she rode off to her castle to await the arrival of a stouter champion.

Night fell; the forest darkened, and Sir Gervais hung in stunned melancholy, pondering the magic and enchantment that had carried him into this high tree after he had so sorely punished the feeble baron.

Then a soft, musical voice called from the forest floor, and, bending down his eyes—for nothing else could he move—he espied the seeming lush and beautiful daughter of the seeming giant, the moonlight shining on her golden-seeming hair and upon her bulging, ripe-seeming breasts.

"I'll have thee down in a trice, handsome knight," she called up.

"Thank . . . you," he muttered between clenched teeth.

"But first, thou must promise me a boon."

"What . . . boon?" he asked with effort.

"Before I dislodge thee from that forked bough, thou must promise . . ." The maiden blushed and turned her face aside.

"Get . . . on . . . with . . . it!" muttered the knight.

"O, how can I say this with modesty? As my father told thee, I am of the runting age. But there is no one in this forest with whom to runt. Ere I dislodge thee from that tree, thou must promise to teach me the ways of runting. There! I have said it!" And she hid her face with her hands and flushed to the tops of her bulging breasts.

"Done . . . and . . . agreed," Sir Gervais rasped between locked teeth.

And with this the seeming sumptuous maid hitched her skirts about her belly in such wise that fud and ecu were bathed in the cool breezes of night, and, arming herself with a stout stick, she lithely scaled the tree and jammed the stick behind the helmet, heaving off with such good will that Sir Gervais was wrenched free and fell with stunning clatter to the earth, where he did sit awhile in a daze.

And know ye that ere his swirling senses returned, the seeming lush maiden was upon him, tugging at the lacings of his armour that he might serve her as he had pledged. And right willing was his brawn to redeem his promise; and often did he mount to this end; but upon each instance, his imaginings did inform him that the moist and panting maid beneath him was, in truth, a loathsom hag the swiving of which was beneath his dignity, and these thoughts did again and again make him limp. For many hours was he by turns stiffened and shrivelled till, near the dawning, he was sore cramped and lamed with dog's cullions from the flowing and ebbing of hard blood.

Then was it that the maiden drew aside and pouted. And she asked, "Is what we have performed this much-praised runting I hear about?"

In his shame and confusion, he attested that they had done the most and the best of runting.

"Nay then," spat out the maiden. "Runting is a thing most treacherously over-famed! If it be for this that maidens sigh and in consequence of which they grow great and make babes to dangle from their teats, then no more of it shall I have! If God protect me from increase upon this occasion, I vow me to a nunnery, there to work His will till my flesh age beyond yearning and temptation."

And Sir Gervais did affirm her in this choice, saying that if she drew not pleasure from *his* swiving, the best and most of the art, then sure lesser men would never please her. And he did feel pride in his heart,

knowing that he had served God by assisting a maiden
to a nunnery, where she would pass her life to lee-
ward of temptation.

And so it was, in the fulness of time, the Maid of
the Enchanted Forest rose from nonne to abbess. And
at last was she hoisted to the high rank of sainte in
reward for abjuring the company and joy of men for
all of the six and eighty years she passed on this earth.
For in her, beauteous, lush, moist, plump, and frick as
she was, celibacy was accounted a miracle; while, in
the generality of nonnes, it is accounted a petty ac-
complishment, as it is no great feat to defend the bul-
warks of chastity when no man undertakes to assail
them by reason of Nature's stern barriers.

As for Sir Gervais, he did wander for a time in the
enchanted forest until he blundered into a greensward through which a merry stream did course. And
there he discovered two knights, one all in black armour and the other all in red, so closely engaged in
working dire hurt upon one another in heavy combat
that they noted not that Gervais stole their horses, one
to ride upon, and the other taken to befuddle pursuit.

In time, he returned to the company of the Table
Round, where he did entertain his comrades with his
tale of passing a year and a day in the enchantment
and arms of a beauteous bespelled maiden princess;
and how he had severely firked and bashed a haughty
baron, feeble of stature and brittle of bone, but forward of talk and bobaunce; and how he had come nigh
to being seduced by an ugly and all-rotted hag who
disguised herself as a moist and frick lass. And all
were amazed at his tale and filled with wonder. And
good Queen Gwenevere was so enthralled that she

did require that Sir Gervais come to her chambers and demonstrate how he had worked upon the enchanted princess. But the queen was slow of comprehension, and Sir Gervais was required to demonstrate many times before she was satisfied in her understanding.

And thus, for all the days of his life, Sir Gervais was affected by the habits of his enchantment and the spells of other-seeming. For ever it was his practice to take to belly only crones and hags full of years and distort of feature. Also did he limit his displays of prowess to the brittle bones of puny peasant grandfathers. And even those who scoffed at the quality of his foes and lovers were constrained to confess that he was more often successful with sword and tool than the generality of men.

And so it was that the fame of Sir Gervais was sung down the corridors of time by bards and minstrels, in the lays and songs of which he was clept Braster of Ancients and Swiver of Crones, and was accounted bravest knight of all, save for him who would one day prove his worth by solving the riddle of the Parlous Seat.

S T A V E   V I I I

*IN WHICH RUDE PERSIVAL, NOW KNIGHT-ERRANT
AND IMPOVERISHED, PASSES THROUGH A TIME
OF INVISIBILITY, BUT SURVIVES TO BECOME
A KNIGHT OF THE TABLE ROUND, THIS
BEING PART THE THIRD: LOW
ADVENTURES AND HIGH.*

 dire enchantment!" pronounced the Baron earnestly, "How perilously close came the noble Sir Gervais to besmirching his noble tool in that foul hag that pretended to be a lush, moist, frick, and beauteous maiden. What a disgrace it would have been for him! But, though his mind was befuddled, his highborn tool shrank from the loathsom task. Is this not proof that nobility is born into the flesh, and has nought to do with the mind, good Sir Launcelot? Ho-hey, fellow knight!" shouted the Baron, shaking the sleeping beggar by his collar. "Lift thy drooping pate from the table! Be awake! Thou hast rested aplenty whilst the fair Elaine entertained us with story-telling. Now is it time to pursue thy tale of Persival the Rude. Nay, do not gasp for air and scrub

thine eyes so! Give over this blinking and gaping! To the tale! To the tale!"

Arh . . . gluck . . . blah . . . ahem . . . and so it was that the young and rude Percy, newly become Sir Persival the Rude through the miracle of Elevation, walked forth upon the green land of England to prove himself a knight, though impoverished. He did wander a year, through the season of mist and fog, through the term of snows, through the period of rain and drip, and through those two days of watery sunlight that in this land are called summer, offering to all he met to perform valorous deeds of close combat to demonstrate his prowess and worth. But as he lacked coin— that being disappeared along with the Old 'Un—he had no armour and was mounted only on shank's mare. So the knights he met upon the road scorned to debase themselves in the combatting of him; and Sir Persival perforce had to content himself with doing battle upon peasants and minstrels, outlaws and strolling players, beggars and artists, and suchlike lees of humanity as fate sent his way. Though the glory and profit of these combats were modest, by dint of numbers and application did Sir Persival slowly fill his slack purse with enough bent farthings to purchase a plow mare which sought to compensate for her lack of saddle by being so sway-backed as to make a comfortable seat, though she could not be ridden over stony ground, lest her belly scrape. For armour he had about his chest a wine barrel with two holes cut in the sides for his arms; and for helm he had a bronze chamber pot strapped beneath his chin.

While wandering in search of glory and suste-

nance it befell that Persival was taken with an ague.
And all dazed and ranting with the fever, he did arrive
at the gate of a nunnery, there seeking hospice and
succour. The goodly nonnes tugged him from his
mare, unstrapped his pisspot helm, and shook him out
of his barrel armour; then they did drag him into the
warmth and comfort of their nunnery, three pulling at
each leg as his head bounced freely upon the cobble-
stones. And it was the pious prioress herself that did
attend him in his fever, bathing his brow with cool
water, and making his members comfortable. During
the performance of these charities, the prioress discovered the secret of Persival's Flaw, which both astonished and het her.

In his fever Persival babbled of his desire to become a formidable and puissant knight that he might
earn a place at the Table Round, and the prioress took
pity on him, for know you that she was so smitten by
the young man that she forgave him his dire and
shameful Flaw.

When, in the passage of time, the fever relented,
she spake soothingly to him, saying, "Fair knight, I
would fain aid thee along thy path to fame and glory,
but the only gift in my power to bestow is but a petty
one, though it might in small way assist thee in combat by bewildering and amazing all opponents. For
know ye, handsome knight, that I have conned the
darker lore and can, through exercise of magic, render
thee all invisible."

Now did Persival's eyes shine at the prospect of
riding forth invisible, that he might approach another
knight all unseen and bash him to the earth of a sudden, while the other was still at the whistling of a
merry air or the pruning of his fingernails with a dag-

ger. So he did supplicate the prioress, begging her to perform upon him the magic rite.

And this did she do, muttering incantations and gasps as she laid hands upon him and touched him here and there, here and there, here and there. As most of her touching was about his Flaw, Persival did blush on her behalf, for he knew that the use and application of that tool was beyond her pious knowledge and experience. At last she drew back, saying, "Now art thou all invisible!"

But Persival did look down and see himself, and he did say, "How can it be that I am all invisible, for I can see right clearly my arms and chest and bulge." But the prioress did laugh lightly, saying, "Tis but thy clothing that thou seest, for know ye that my spell extends only to the flesh. If thou wouldst doff thy clothing, then wouldst thou be as invisible and insubstantial as the thin air or the piety of a bishop. And fear not to blush me with thy nudity and shame my virgin eye, for know ye that, without thy clothes, there is nothing shameful that I could see."

And Persival doff'd his clothes and stood before her dressed as he was at birth.

The prioress glanced about the chamber, at him and away from him, and she frowned and said, "Nay, fair knight, whither hast thou gone? Speak, that I might know where thou standest." And she did grope out blindly and grasp him. "Ah, I have thee by the wrist, good knight, and I shall hold thee that I might know where thou art."

Now Persival knew well that she held not his wrist, but he durst not enlighten her, lest she wither in shame.

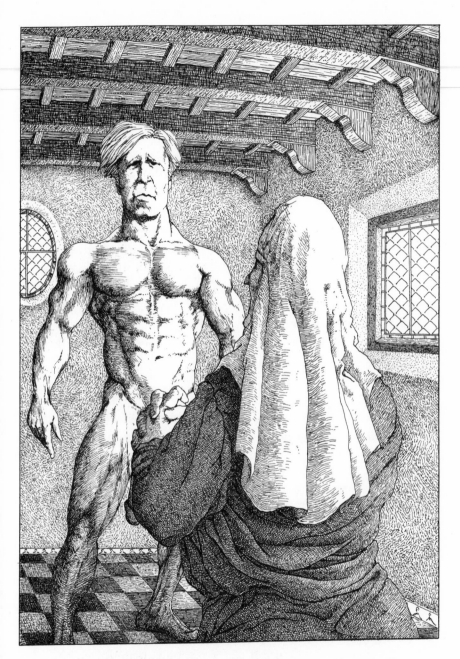

"AND PERCIVAL DOFF'D HIS CLOTHES AND STOOD BEFORE HER
DRESSED AS HE WAS AT BIRTH."

"But stay," he said, "how can it be that I am all invisible? For know ye that when I look down I do see my very chest, and belly, and . . . wrist."

"La, la," laughed the prioress, stroking the childish knight's wrist playfully. "Thine error is common to those but newly invisible. Dost thou not comprehend that thine invisible eyes can see thine invisible flesh all clearly, while my visible eyes can in no wise see that which is invisible? Now sit here beside me and tell me how thou plottest to use thine invisibility to become a knight of wide fame and repute." And she did draw him to sit beside her and did hold his wrist in her lap as they parleyed. "Nay, good knight, be not ill at ease and nervous with me, nor flex thy wrist so in anxiety. Hm-m-m, now I bethink myself, this is not thy wrist I hold, for surely this must be thy forearm."

"Yea, e'en so, good nonne," said Sir Persival, shamed and disgraced that his wrist had become a forearm in the hands of this goodly nonne who, in her virgin innocence, knew not what she held and stroked. Yet, for all his shame, he could not master his ardour, though he blushed at it and promised to do harsh penance.

Then did the prioress rise, saying, "It is time, my invisible knight, for thee to quit me that I might attend to my prayers and the humiliation of my flesh. So leave me, for it would not be modest and meet that a man be by whilst I humiliate and humble my flesh no matter what degree of invisibility he has achieved." And with this she released Persival's forearm and, going to the door of her chamber, opened it that he might leave. But so quickly did she close the door and draw the bolts that Persival was still within the room when the prioress turned back into the chamber, muttering to herself, "How glad I am to be alone, for in modesty I would not have that knight, handsome though he be, know that in deep piety I do mortify my flesh all nude." And with this she quickly doff'd her clothing and stood in the middle of the chamber in the raiment of Eve.

Then did Sir Persival press against the wall and breathe softly that he might not shame this holy woman who thought herself all alone and privy, and he did avert his eyes as she threw herself upon her low cot and grasped at her breasts, kneading and pulling at them as though she would rid herself of these worldly temptations. And then, writhing in the agony of her sin, she began to elevate the soul through the mortification of the miserable flesh, and did begin to abuse herself right vigourously.

Now know ye that within Persival's mind a great combat raged between his earnest desire to protect this holy woman, and the calls of his manhood. The victory, trist to relate, went ultimately to the flesh, and he did approach the writhing and moaning prioress.

"Ah! What be this?" quoth the prioress to herself. "Is this the weight of my sins I feel pressing me down? Be this a demon tormenting me? Or be this a miracle? Nay! More like it is a devil come to tempt me, an all-unseen incubus bent upon having me! God give me strength to struggle against him, and grapple with him, and push him from me!"

Grapple and push the good woman did for more than an hour. And in her torment she did moan and grasp and clench her teeth and writhe and heave and seek to subdue her tormentor with fingernails to his nape and with efforts to squeeze the very life out of it with her thighs. And her labours were not in vain, for at last the demon fell weak and limp and withdrew. But her victory was transitory, as it was not long before the incubus came again to torment her, and through all of that long night she did struggle, pitting all the strength of her grace and holiness against this terrible thing.

And when at last dawn was at her casement, she knew that the forces of good had vanquished those of evil, for never before had her flesh been so mortified. And there was a great peace and calm within her, and she fell into the deep sleep of the righteous and pure.

And invisible Persival retired to a corner of the rude chamber, where he sat against the wall and fell into the deep sleep of the evil and naughty.

With morn, the prioress awoke and left her pallet to attend to her duties, in the course of which all the younger nonnes did remark that, although she walked with some difficulty and stiffness in stigma of her religious performances, yet about her was a smiling and gentle aura as of one who has known the testing and victory of that divine grace that overcomes all evil.

Now, when he awoke, Persival felt a great hunger upon him by cause of having so lately risen from a bed of fever and also by cause of his labours of that night; and he decided to break his fast with the nonnes in the refectory. To this end, he was about donning his clothes when he bethought himself better of it. "Nay, my lad! It would not do to give fright and start to these good women by having an empty suit of clothes suddenly appear amongst them to take food. They will think thee a ghost. Go thou to dine all nude, that thou mightest avoid stunning and shocking the nonnes."

And so it was that Persival yode him to the refectory. And when he entered, there were a full score of nonnes seated at the long table with the prioress, and one place was in readiness before an empty chair. Now know you that, upon the moment of his entrance, Persival did in some small way doubt the thoroughness of his invisibility, for all eating and converse did stop of a sudden, and thin gruel did drip from wooden spoons frozen inches from gaping mouths and did fall into laps with the soft pattering of autumn rain upon the leaves. But just as Persival covered his face with his hands to hide his shame, of an instant did all eating and talk recommence with suddenness and vigour, and he did overhear one nonne say to another that twas pity the impoverished knight they had taken in to cure of his fever had not yet the strength to join them in the breaking of their fasts.

And so it was with light heart that Persival sat upon the empty stool and began with great appetite to consume his bowl of gruel.

Then it was that the prioress spake out, saying, "Ah, young knight, I perceive that thou hast joined us and are mended from thy fever in such wise as to gobble up thy gruel with great vigour. For know ye that, while your parts and body are all invisible to mine eye, yet do I see thy wooden spoon rise from thy bowl into space and back again, and therefore do I, through deduction and logick, assume that thou art amongst us, else why would thy spoon act in this antick way?"

Then was it that each nonne in turn did greet the

invisible knight, wishing him most cheerily a good morrow; and the oldest amongst them, who had, in youth, sacrificed her beauty and charm to Christ in the hope that it was not the paltriness of the gift that mattered, but the spirit in which it was foisted, spake out in the direction of the rising and falling spoon, saying, "Know ye, fair knight, that our good prioress convened us together this morn and told us of thy wonderous affliction, and how thou art beneath a spell of invisibility in such wise that all who are good and chaste cannot see thee in the slightest, while any who harbour lustful and low thoughts can see with perfect clarity, for thy body is beyond the seeing and comprehension of good Christians, as are so many things in this world. And I confess to thee, handsome knight, that many of us were some afeared at thine arrival to the refectory, lest we, in the imperfection of our piety, should be cursed with the ability to see thee. I, for one, do attest—although I scorn the sin of pride—that I am right content and grateful that the good Lord hath given me the purity of soul that prevents me from seeing thy handsome face, strong chest, wide shoulders, and huge . . . appetite."

And in a babble of voices, each striving to be first, all the nonnes did aver that they too were relieved to find the handsome knight invisible to their eyes.

And the repast did continue with much talk of enchantments and miracles the like of which the nonnes had observed in the past. And they did speak of ghosts and spirits of the damned that were known to infest this very nunnery. And one nonne did regale the others with a story of recent ghostly infection, saying that upon a dark and stormy night she had heard low moans in the cell next to hers, and had been greatly affrighted, yet she had summoned the courage to seek out the source of this ghostly sound, and she had crept down the hall and had entered stealthily into the cell of a young novice newly arrived to the nunnery. And lo! In the darkness the uneasy ghost of some long-dead nonne rustled past her in the doorway! And when she struck light, she did find the young novice upon her pallet, so tormented by the apparition of the ghost that she had thrown off her habit in confusion and was in stark and awful nudity, dazed and supine! And for some hours did the novice continue thus writhing and moaning low in her amazement and torment, although the nonne did administer to her wants with great gentleness and devotion as women know best how to do.

And by turns did each nonne have a like story to tell, and they did affright themselves and one another with the telling of them in such wise that, in their fear, they clung and clutched at each other.

Now know you that young Persival was right pleased with this proof of his invisibility, and he did enjoy the company of these pious nonnes, although he took pity on one who sat opposite him, for she was afflicted with great clumsiness in such wise that thrice she did drop her spoon to the floor and had to crawl under the table to retrieve it, and in her clumsy grappling for it did oft and again grasp his invisible Flaw.

To the end of regaining his strength that he might ride forth to do harsh and noble deeds, young Sir Persival abode four weeks in that nunnery, but far from recovering from the fatigues of his fever, his strength did seem to ebb with each passing day. For it must be confessed that young Persival took to the habit of testing his invisibility in one cell or another each night, and though the enchantment proved itself each time, yet did devilish ill chance cause each nonne in her turn to blunder in amazement upon his Flaw and, not understanding the nature of this invisible presence, each did struggle to subdue it in the way she thought best.

So it was that young Persival bethought him to quit the company of these good and pious women ere his strength be gone altogether. And when he left the nunnery astride his sway-backed mare, he did so wearing neither pisspot helmet nor wine-cask armour, but all nude, for he plotted to amaze and overwhelm such errant knights as he encountered along the way, for they would be little prepared for attack by a riderless mare.

And know ye that to this day the pisspot and cask are enshrined there as holy relicks, the Grail and Casket of the Chapel of Our Lady of the Invisible Joy.

Many were the mishaps that befell young Persival, for full a score of times he did approach upon the road a full-armoured knight. And as he neared, Sir Persival would chuckle softly behind his hand in anticipation of the bewilderment the poor knight would know when, after watching with wonder the approach of a riderless mare to the very side of him, he would suddenly feel himself tugged by unseen hands from his saddle and beaten roundly with his own weapons.

And indeed the knights did stare in amazement to see themselves approached by a bare-arsed youth upon a sway-backed mare, his member dangling almost to the dust. But things did not proceed as Sir

Persival had hoped. For upon each occasion, just as he slipped from the mare's back and crept to the side of the knight to tug him from the saddle, that knight would disembarrass himself of the nuisance with a casual bash of his mace, or a rearmain of his steel gauntlet, or the flat of his sword, or the toe of his boot. And the knight would ride off, disdaining to do greater hurt to an idiot.

But, as he sat all dazed in the dust, the Invisible Knight would shout after the departing foe, "Think not thou hast gained glory by this combat, cur! For know ye that thou hast revealed thyself to be an impure and lustful man by being able to see me sneak up on thee! Shame upon thee! Shame, shame, double shame!"

And the departing knight would shake his head sorrowfully and ride on.

Thus was it that, after a time of wandering, Sir Persival found himself one morn at the gates of towering Camelot, where he sat, bare of arse, elbow, and pissette, upon his sway-backed horse, shivering in the dawn wind.

"Yo-ho, the castle!" he cried. "Drop bridge and raise portcullis! For know ye that there is a knight-errant astride this charger, though such of you as are pure of spirit and all unsinful can see him not!"

And several of the knight-fellows of the Table Round yode them to the parapet and looked down upon the naked knight, his skin all blue and bumpled with the cold.

"Nay, madcap idiot," called down Sir Gervais,

Braster of Ancients and Swiver of Crones. "Get thee hence, nor continue to display thy blue and bumpled arse to the cringing eyes of our ladyfolk, unless thou yearnest to feel my mace upon thy temple!"

"I demand the hospitality due a knight, by the lamenting balls of Job! And if thou givest it not, then prepare to send down a champion to defend thy scant honour! For know ye that thou hast confessed thyself a bag of lust and sin by being able to see my blue and bumpled arse!"

Then laughed Sir Bohort, he of the Wonderous Feat. "Be off, bare-arsed fool, lest I grapple thee to my chest and do my wonderous feats till thou dost gasp and swoon!" For know you that Sir Bohort had taken to the use of his feat in close combat, and a dire weapon it had proven to be.

Then did Queen Gwenevere come to discover the source of this merriment, and she did look down upon Sir Persival the Rude. Then, speaking to Sir Gay, who stood beside her, she said in a hushed and choked voice, "My God! Is that what I wit it to be, dangling down the side of the mare, e'en nigh unto the ground?"

And Sir Gay did gulp and gasp. "Good my queen, I find myself also gawking at this with some amazement."

And the two did almost swoon limp into each other's arms.

Then came King Arthur to the parapet, scrubbing the sleep from his eyes and frowning heavily at the din and bruit that had broken his rest. "Will none of my knights punish this rogue who is so brazen as to yelp up at us whilst he sits there exposed to wind and eye?"

Then did I, who was brave Sir Launcelot in those lost and lamented days, stride forward, proud of stature, handsome beyond all others, dignified yet warlike, my golden locks streaming in the morning breeze, my fine clear eyes ablaze with courage, yet gentle and profound, my voice rich and mellow, my speech ever decorated with wisdom and deep learning, my manner firm but kind, my—

"For God's sake, get on with it!" demanded the Baron.

Ah, yes. Forgive me. Well . . . then did I stride to the parapet and ask the good Queen Gwenevere what matter this was that brought my fellow knights to shouting and jeering. And when I espied the pitiful lad, nude and blue with cold, astride his miserable mare, I called down, warning him to betake himself elsewhere and bother us no further, lest he suffer the instruction of my sword. But that foul and ill-bred scroff cried back that I must be low and lust-besmirched to be able to see him, and he did challenge me to combat, swearing upon the nether parts of two saints and a pope.

Laughter rippled my manly voice and scorn invaded my clear azure eyes as I turned away, not deigning to blot my history of brave battles with the gore of this shivering, bare-arsed lout. And I strode off, dignity and high manhood revealed in my every step, my locks of spun gold lifted lightly in the breeze, my mind deep in sage and clever thoughts, my—

The Baron cleared his throat meaningfully.

Ah, yes. Do excuse me. Well . . . as I strode away, my fellow knights laughed at me, claiming that I was afeared to face this impudent swine in manly combat. My noble ire rose to this, and I vowed to give the lie to those who insulted me thus. And with this I went off to make ready for the combat, donning my fullest armour.

As I was readying myself for battle, Queen Gwenevere and Sir Gay visited me privily, supplicating that I limit my blows to the upper part of the rogue's body. This slight boon I granted them freely as, setting foot to stirrup, I called to have the drawbridge lowered.

Then was it that several of the jocular knights of the Table Round came to me, jeering and asking if I thought I had steel enough about my body to dare face a bare-arsed bumpkin. And one of them snickered and asked what disposal should be made of my armour, should the stranger knight upset, bash, and do for me. And all of them did laugh at this thin jest. Then was it that my stung pride prompted me to my ultimate downfall, for in my haughtiness I responded, saying, "Scoff not, fellow knights! And hear this! Should I fail to defeat yonder shivering scamp, then let me be condemned to wander forever the roads and byways, a low beggar and scornworthy." And with this terrible oath, I rode forth.

I must recount the next happenings as I learned them later, for at the time my mind was all a-muddle and unclear.

Riding out, I found the naked fool upon the sward beyond the castle walls. But as I set my lance well into its rest and bore down upon him, the recreant lout snatched his mare about by her ears and fled at all speed, his bare arse bounding right desperately upon her bony spine. It was to the target of this dancing moon that I directed the point of my lance as I charged after him, the distance between us ever decreasing until the steel point was but inches from making him howl right vigourously. And at this instant did we break together into the forest, and he clung low upon the back of his mount, while I sat proud and upright upon my noble charger. So it was that he passed unscathed beneath a stout overhanging bough, while I took the branch full in the chest and, with a splintering crash, rolled over my steed's fud and clattered to the ground. Then did the beggardly bastard rein up his mare by her ears and sit astride, watching my dazed efforts with galling amusement, as I struggled to my feet and reeled dizzily, my flesh all a-tingle with the shock. Then I stumbled over a stone and crashed again to the ground, earning myself a mighty blow to the visor that bent it in such wise that I could neither see through it nor raise it. Again did I bravely strive to my feet and, all dazed, essay to draw out my sword, but I cut my hand deep with it and, yowling, cast it down and kicked at it in rage, bashing my foot on a boulder to the laming of it. Then did the bastard's laughter madden me, though I could see nothing of him. I rushed towards the sound of his scornful laugh, my head down apurpose to drive my helm deep into the coward's belly.

Little did I know he was standing behind a tree.

When my swimming senses returned somewhat, I put forth heroic effort and strove again to my feet. With numb fingers, I took the chain mace from my girdle and staggered forward, swinging it so as to imperil all the space about me, for nothing could I see. And with such force did I swing that dire weapon that the barbed head sang a low moan through the air, and the chain links stood stiff and straight.

But, trist-o-dear,* the chain wrapped over a branch, and the ball whipped around and delivered me a blow to the helm that quite dropped me to my knees, deafened, stunned, and defeated.

"I yield me, bare-arsed knight!" I gasped out. "I do aver that never in all my jousts and combats have I met so cunning and quick an adversary. Truly thou dost merit to be amongst that noble company of the Table Round."

And thus it was, my good host, that Persival the Rude became the last fellow of the Table Round, while I . . . ah, woe! . . . was condemned by the terms of my terrible oath to roam the roads for all time, a beggar and despised. Yea, e'en to sink so low as to

---

* This peculiar expletive appears nowhere else in fourteenth-century literature, but one of my scholar ancestors has suggested that it might derive from the French for "sad to say." —N.S.

end with telling crude tales in the hall of an ignorant petty noble in some miserable corner of Wales!

And with this the clapperdudgeon-knight's eyes filled with tears, and he bowed his head in grief.

S T A V E   IX

he Baron was silent for a time, his mind clouded with an effort to comprehend something the beggar had just said. "What was that bit about petty, ignorant nobles and miserable corners of Wales?" He fixed a squinting eye on the dejected tale-weaver. "Wouldst care to cast some light on that part?"

"Ah-h . . . well . . . one might put it . . . that is . . ."

But the fair Elaine came to her fellow's aid, saying, "Truly, mine host, any light good Launcelot might cast would be feeble against that which Nature even now casts into the world, for look ye through the casement and see how Night has flown, and Dawn with a red rag about her shoulders is tramping all wet-footed over the hills to the east.* So the hour has come that we must be on our way."

"What sayest thou? Is the tale-spinning done, then?"

"Yea, e'en so, brother knight," said ancient Launcelot. "My lady and I must commit ourselves to the road, the cold, and the morrow. Such is the nature and condition of our curse."

"Yea, but . . ." The Baron's eyes grew large and his lip trembled at the thought that the tales were at an end. "But what of the Parlous Seat thou hast mentioned again and again? Was it Persival that was chosen to break its spell? Did he sit in it without hurt?"

"Nay, brother, for know ye that Persival was given mine own seat to the Table Round, when I was cast out to wander the roads."

"But God damn it, what was the purpose of thy mentioning oft and oft the shitlicking chair, an thou hast no story upon it?"

"O, there is a story! A right wonderous story. Long of durance and rude of detail. With fighting and foining, with valour and lust."

"Ah! Let's have it then," the Baron said, pressing the two back into their places and filling their cups to the brims.

"Nay, nay, brother knight. Tis a tale for another season, when our wanderings carry us again to this desolate corner of the realm. Now we must be upon

---

* Over the years, several scholars of my family have noted that this line appears in *Hamlet:* I,i,166, albeit in a somewhat overly refined version. We are not prepared to suggest direct plagiarism. After all, coincidences of poetic inspiration do occur. —N.S.

our way. But fear not to miss the rare fine tale, for it is our practice to return to such gracious hosts as have given us warm clothes against the weather and stout mounts to lighten our journey."

"But I have given thee no such things!"

"O?" said the beggar-knight, his eyes round with surprise. "Hast thou not? Ah, tis pity then. Tis pity. For the tale must go all untold and unheard."

"Must it? O, must it?"

"But be strong, brother. Life consists not only of rare lusty tales of nonnes and knights, of battle and swiving, of magic and romance. There be grander and finer things in the world than these."

"Such as . . . ?"

"Well, such as charity, nobility, kindness, honesty, bravery, compassion, constancy, piety, sincerity, friendship—"

"O, a devil's piss on such trifles! It's tales I want! I need tales!" And the Baron clutched the beggar by his shoulders and said, "Color my days, for God's sake! You see . . ." He glanced about to assure himself that his wife and his daughter dozing at the table could not overhear him, and he lowered his voice. "You see, brother knight, I have begun to grow old."

"Say it not!"

"Well, a little old. A *little* old. And life has turned out to be somewhat less than I had in mind when I was young and all was possible. I haven't accomplished much, you see. A man without memories must have tales. Canst understand that?"

The old beggar looked upon his host as something other than prey for the first time. "Yes," he said. "I can understand that. The great gap twixt tawdry

Here-and-Now and rosy Might-Have-Been, that is the span across which the story-teller weaves his gossamer bridges."

"Look ye, I know that I am tardy in my generosity, but what if I set to providing you with stout mounts and warm clothes, wouldst thou then come back next winter and—"

"Done!"

"What cheer! What hope! Ah, to know there will be stories to warm next winter!" Of a sudden, the Baron leapt up, the hairs standing on his nape. "Aghah! What is that spectre in the shadows of the hall? Dost see that limp and hollow ghost that creeps towards us, its eyes all sunken and its face so pale and drawn? My sword! I shall defend us against this ghastly apparition! My sword! . . . and perhaps a cross."

"Nay, Father," said the waking daughter. "'Tis but the young priest descending from the shriving place."

"How? What? This horrid thing that reels and totters, that gasps and gawks, that shuffles and limps, that stares and shivers, can this be the handsome and strengthy priest who erst beamed and smiled upon us, all composure and civility, though he had no ripe tales to tell, but only dreary stories of soul's betterment that were not worth a fig? Can this be he?"

"E'en so, my husband," said the waking wife as she assisted the priest to the table, his weight upon her frail shoulder.

"Poor lad," lamented the Baron. "There hast thou a lesson in excess of zeal, my friends. Piety, like honesty, is a precious thing not to be wasted wantonly when there is no vantage to be gained. But enough of this high wisdom and philosophy. The dawn is come, and my bed beckons. And our guests have said they must be on their way. So all of you out! Begone, begone all guests . . . though I say it with all warm hospitality."

The storm had passed, and the first yellow sun slanted across virgin fields of eye-squinting white as the guests made their ways from the castle of Dolbadarn, Launcelot and his Elaine going up the road, and the priest staggering down, the mules of the first poking round holes of blue shadow in the snow, and the heavy feet of the latter dragging out great scoops as he reeled and floundered his way home.

The Baron and his wife stood at the casement, watching their guests depart. With a yawn of deep satisfaction, the Baron said, "Know ye, wife, that things are not always as they seem. For look ye there at the departing Launcelot and his fair maiden, all bundled against Nature with robes and furs, astride sleek fat mules. But a few hours ago, one might have taken them for scrofulous beggars scratching at the door for alms and orts. But see now how fine and noble a picture they make, sitting high-chinned and proud upon their mounts! Now turn thine eyes to the departing priest! But a night ago, I took him for a handsome and brawny fellow of youth and vigour. But see him now! Far gone. Far gone is he towards age and decrepitude. Nay, wife, nay. Things are not always what they seem, even when they seem to be."

And the Baron chuckled to himself and placed his

hand upon his wife's haunch. "And something further, my wife. All this wine in my blood and all these tales of foining and swiving in my brain have rearmed me some in such wise that I might have a surprise for thee in our chambers. So to bed, wife. To bed." He winked and chortled. "But perhaps not to sleep."

And they yode them to their chambers.

The great hall was empty and without sound, save for the crack and tinkle of icicles that fell from the eaves to the stone courtyard, their grip weakened by the touch of the sun. And the clash and clatter of ice upon stone had something of the ring of steel upon steel, as though two knights, one perhaps caparisoned all in black, the other perhaps all in scarlet, did work towards glory, battling sans end upon some greensward through which a merry stream might course.

—fin—

*"THE BARON AND HIS WIFE STOOD AT THE CASEMENT,
WATCHING THEIR GUESTS DEPART."*

GLOSSARY

AS THE READER can judge from a glance at the swatch of the original manuscript that ends the Preface, a direct transcription of my ancestor's words would have made heavy going. So it was necessary to modernize the language. At the same time, I chose to retain certain usages and words that seemed to preserve the flavour and tone of the original. Still, it might be a service to the curious to provide a brief glossary of the more archaic terms and usages, and this I do willingly.

AN, conj.   If.

AVOID, v.   To empty; hence, to avoid the saddle is to dismount.

BLESSURE, n.   Wound. (Note: This word, like many others in this glossary, comes directly from the French, which is not surprising, as the manuscript was written only three hundred years after the Battle of Hastings.)

BOBAUNCE, n.   *Madness; insanity; foolishness.*

BRAST, pp.   *Broken.*

BRENT, pp.   *Burnt.*

BRUIT, n. & v.   *Noise; in some usages, rumour. To announce; to spread rumour.*

CACHE, v.   *To hide; to conceal.*

CAITIFF, adj.   *Mean; base; despicable.*

CAITIFHEDE, n.   *Meanness; baseness; lowness.*

CAP-A-PIE, adv.   *Head-to-toe.*

CLAPPERDUDGEON, n.   *A born beggar.*

CLEPT, pp.   *Named; called.*

CUL, n.   *Buttocks; anus.*

CULLIONS, n.   *Testicles. (See Dog's Cullions.)*

DIZAINE, n.   *Ten or so.*

DOG'S CULLIONS, n.   *A local discomfort deriving from repeated arousal without satisfaction. (See Cullions.)*

DRETCH, n.   *Torment; pain. In some usages, trouble.*

DUNGMUNCHING, adj.   *Poetic embellishment on "shitlicking" (q.v.)*

ECOUTE, v.   *Harken; listen here.*

ECU, n.   *Shield. By extension, the shield-shaped pubes of a woman.*

ERSTER, adv.   *Yet earlier.*

FAGGOT, n.   *Bundle.*

FARDEL, n.   *Burden.*

FEWTER, n.   *Lance socket.*

FFRIDD, n.   *Stone wall in Welsh sheep country.*

FIG, n.   *Digital gesture of rude and uncomplimentary implication.*

FIRK, v.   *To beat.*

FLEAK, n.   A most pejorative term for a woman, suggestion a penchant for horizontality not mitigated by a penchant for cleanliness.

FOIN, v.   In fencing, to attack with the point of the sword. By poetic extension, to make love.

FRICK, adj.   Lusty; full-blooded; not averse to romantic encounter.

FUD, n.   Buttocks.

GRAMERCY.   Thank you.

GREDE, v.   To wail; to complain.

HET, pp.   Made warm or hot.

HIGHT, pp.   Named; called.

JOLI, adj.   Pretty; fine.

LAIDLY, adj.   Ugly.

LESING, n.   Error or omission.

LET, v.   To prevent.

LEWD, adj.   Unlettered or ignorant.

LICKSHIT, adj. & n.   Servile or base. A broad and general pejorative, much of its piquancy drained through over-use. As noun: A base or servile person.

LIT, n.   Bed. A direct borrow from the French, found only in the phrase, "lists and lits," as in: "He was strong (or weak) in lists and lits," meaning in combat and in love-making.

MAUGRE, prep.   Despite.

MAUNDER, v.   To talk in a dreamy or foolish manner.

MEET, adj.   Proper or appropriate.

NI FIG NI FART, idiom.   Very little; nothing at all. The "ni . . . ni . . ." structure here is a direct borrow from the French, meaning "neither . . . nor . . ." (Note: It would appear that "fig" [q.v.] is here

used as though the gesture were the event suggested.)
I confess that the expression of the Baron in which
this ancient idiom appears (p. 115) has stood me in
good stead when, during my years as an academic,
I found myself besieged at social gatherings by
young scholars of literature who felt duty-bound to
discover a symbolic level beneath everything, and
yet more duty-bound to tell you about it.

PAWKY, adj.   Sly or clever. (Scots employ the term to
describe a national characteristic which they find
pertly attractive, and which the English find a
damned nuisance.)

PAYNIM, adj.   Pagan. More broadly, non-Christian.

PINGLE, v.   To pick at one's food.

PISSETTE, n.   Penis.

PRETE, adj.   Ready or prepared.

QUETCH, v.   To twitch or to wince, as in pain or,
upon particular occasions, in pleasure. (Note: Together with an old friend and Yiddish scholar, I once
sought out the relation of this word to "Kvetch." We
could trace "Quetch" to the Old Saxon Quekilik,
but though we knew that Old Saxon and Yiddish
both derive from the West Germanic, we were unable
to isolate the common root.)

QUOP, v.   To throb or beat.

REARMAIN, n.   A backhand blow.

ROOD, n.   Cross. Usually, the cross of the Crucifixion.

SHITPORT, n.   Anus. (Poetic dysphemism.)

SHITTEN, adj.   Soiled, dirty.

TRISTLY, adv.   Sadly.

VAIR, n.   A variety of ermine. (Note: It may interest

the Reader to know that an ancient fairy tale im-
ported from France spoke of shoes of ermine [*vair*]
which were mistranslated as shoes of glass [*verre*].
On the other hand, it may not.)

WIGHT, adj.   *Courageous or strong.*
WIT, v.   *To know.*
WOOD, adj.   *Mad or insane; foolish.*
WOT, pp.   *Past tence of "wit" (q.v.).*
YODE, pp.   *Went.*